STELLA CARR RIBEIRO was born in Guanabara, Brazil, and now lives and works in São Paulo. She comes from a long line of writers and journalists and was formerly the director and vice president of the Brazilian Union of Writers. A poet, journalist, and author of children's literature, Stella Carr Ribeiro published her first novel, *SAMBAQUI*, in Brazil in 1975. This highly acclaimed work is based on one of the great passions of her life: anthropology, which she studied under the well-known scholar Paulo Duarte.

SAMBAQUI: A NOVEL OF PRE-HISTORY

Stella Carr Ribeiro

Translated by
Claudia Van der Heuvel

 A BARD BOOK/PUBLISHED BY AVON BOOKS

Originally published as *O Homem do Sambaqui: Una Estória na Pré-história* by Edicões Quiron.

AVON BOOKS
A division of
The Hearst Corporation
1790 Broadway
New York, New York 10019

Copyright © 1975 by Stella Carr
English translation copyright © 1987 by Claudia Van der Heuvel
Published by arrangement with the author
Library of Congress Catalog Card Number: 85-91175
ISBN: 0-380-89624-9

First Bard Printing: March 1987

BARD TRADEMARK REG. U.S. PAT. OFF. AND IN OTHER COUNTRIES, MARCA REGISTRADA, HECHO EN U.S.A.

Printed in the U.S.A.

OPM   10   9   8   7   6   5   4   3   2   1

to Paulo Duarte
teacher and friend

*It is necessary to understand a being with respect
to itself and not with respect to me.*

To grasp reality it is first necessary to dismiss experience.

C. Lévi-Strauss

Chapter 1

The man and the woman = the great discovery. And other lesser ones. The thinking that figures out things. How the village lives. The great-blue-animal. Good and evil spirits. The Council of Old Men.

Karincai saw what was left of the day creeping past in the sky tinged with red. He rapidly piled up oysters before the mouth-of-darkness let its throat go along the rocks to swallow the afternoon.

The white-eye of night was closed at that time. It would take more days than the fingers on Karincai's hand before the white-eye would open slowly, a tiny bit at a time, until it became round. The round eye up there in the sky allowed them to collect oysters in the white foam of the angry-water during a cooler time, during the night. The days scalded the soles of their feet, made salt emerge from their bodies, and afflicted their mouths with the desire for water-from-the-stones.

Karincai, as well as many other men of the village, had the work of fishing for oysters, mussels, and other mollusks. Malaí brought him containers of water-from-the-stones. Sometimes be-

1

tween one dive and another, while he sat on a rock at the edge of
the crashing angry-water, Karincai dared to turn his head toward
some incredible thoughts:

"Water, water, water; it goes way up to the sky, far away, very,
very far indeed! Malaí knows stories, everybody knows them;
there are people in places far beyond the beyond."

But that was no more than faith. Karincai was stubborn about
faith, and gave his own direction to his thoughts. When the sky
carried and then spilled its gourds over the earth, Karincai
climbed up the tallest mound of oyster shells. As he let the water
splash all over his face, he formed thoughts about all that. It was
not the anger of the Spirit-of-Evil showing his annoyance, because during the day Karincai saw the eye-of-fire calling the
angry-water on high, saw it rising in light smoke, and saw it
gradually coming together up there.

"Don't ever talk of things like that in the village," Malaí told
him, "because the Council of Old Men will feed you to the wild
animals if you do!"

Karincai sensed the great distance from Malaí, and his mouth
was dry.

The mouth-of-darkness opened, blowing out its breath. Karincai began to think about what it could be, that force which sometimes moved things. One day Malaí's hair had run around her
head so much that it seemed like a devil let loose! And the sand
had run around itself. Karincai had wanted a thought from his
head for this power, but Malaí had pulled him by the arm into the
cave, where the breath could not reach, and there she had run
over his body with her warm lips. Karincai had no longer wanted
to think. Malaí had a body like the sky over the white-sand just
before night, because the sky before night is a yellowish red, like
the skin of everybody. Karincai thought: "Why don't people have
skin of different colors, like the wild animals? Yellows, blues,
greens—not white, that would be very ugly."

Karincai was always thinking about things; he did not accept
the word of the Council. He worked on an idea when he encountered anything, searching for its own reason, while he dug up tree
roots to shape gourds, or was busy making containers.

While Karincai carried the shells to the village the darkness
became complete.

* * *

The water-from-the-stones had a sweet taste; it took the burning from the mouth and returned energy to the body. It came down merrily, singing. Malaí imitated its song with a voice from her throat.

Malaí's hair was long and straight, and sometimes, putting down her water jug, she wet her hair in the water-from-the-stones. Her whole body shivered and she laughed; she laughed a great deal. Malaí loved the green of everything—it made her want to eat. Malaí loved the water running on her body, the soft yellowish red of young skin, the two dark buds growing between her long hair, the bird jumping within her (Karincai's hand always listened to it), and two restless mounds between her hair (smooth, smooth). Malaí was sweet like the water-from-the-stones. Karincai was bold, like the faraway-water that touched the dark blue sky. Karincai was long and fierce like the angry-water where the shells hid.

Malaí thought about herself and about Karincai, about the differences. The water-from-the-stones ran, tickling Malaí. She could never quite fit Karincai into an idea—he was different from the men of the village. Karincai was an almost frightening mystery!

Malaí came from the midst of the stones with her jug full. She wandered in a vague and uncertain way along the soft green of the ground, not quite deciding to return to the village.

The red tongue of the dark mouth was already licking the sky. Malaí had to arrive back at the village before the colors fled from things. Karincai said that the colors did not flee, they only gathered themselves into things. Malaí let Karincai talk only because he spoke well, and she let him say anything he wanted. When he spoke he breathed gently into Malaí's ear, and she nodded yes. He thought that was for his ideas, but it was really for him.

The colored-eyes of the green-plants made it nice to inhale. Malaí stopped for a moment and let the sweet-breath of the colored-eyes of the green-plants enter her breast. The green-plants had eyes of many colors: blues, reds, whites, yellows. Karincai strung them on fibers from tree trunks and decorated Malaí's neck. The eyes of the plants closed quickly. Malaí wanted to save her ornaments for a long time. Karincai promised that he would use his new bamboo pole with a sharpened point to stab the first fierce-blue-fish which lost itself in the shallow-waters of the inlet. He would take out its teeth and make with them an ornament which would last for time without end.

The men of the village did not have, as Karincai had, hands that brought beauty from within things. It was he who had taught the women of the tribe the whimsy of drawing designs on their cups and gourds, and of polishing them until they were smooth. He had also taught them a variety of unfamiliar, elegant shapes for containers, which he said were customary for his father's father's fathers, who came from far away high in the hills. They came from a place where the houses were built on the trunks of trees at a great still pool of water-to-drink. They speared fish with long poles with sharpened fragments on the tips, which could kill even the large animals which suckle!

The young men of the village listened with big-ears; the old men squatted a distance away, pretending not to listen, but everyone knew they were entranced by his words.

The hands of the women began to awaken a festival of designs from their sleep on bowls and cups made from tree trunks. The women all showed their teeth to Karincai, in the most perfect happiness.

Malaí felt an evil-spirit inside her wanting to destroy the young women's bowls, which emerged prettily from their hands for Karincai's eyes. She stayed away, looking from behind a long, wide leaf, her face wrinkled up like a withered fruit, wanting to break things. In her hands was only a bowl, a plain bowl, without beauty, full of water-from-the-stones. Malaí stifled the hurt that entered her throat, and threw to the ground the full gourd, which splattered about in a big rolling fall.

Karincai had still not seen Malaí separate from the other women. This day a strange spirit dressed Malaí's body as she was standing on an enormous rock which was only a shadow, with the immense fire of day burning behind it. It looked as though smoke came from Malaí's golden skin; Malaí's long legs, her arms, and her face were a secret to Karincai's clouded eyes.

The young man made from a piece of wood a long shape like a shaft. Polishing the smooth roundness of the outlines of the soft stick, he made something appear: a strange piece without use or utility, neither gourd nor cup, but only a strange figure without a face, scarcely finished because the sparkle of fire changed Malaí so, and because he was stunned.

The elongated figure remained hidden among the trees for a long day. When the afternoon snuffed out the fire from Malaí's body and the whiteness of night made the girl's gestures become gentle, Karincai gave the statue to Malaí, without a word.

The whole village surrounded the strange piece with questions. Some noticed that it looked like Malaí's long shape; others laughed. "What good is it?" asked many.

The bird within Malaí's body was free; it fluttered against her rounded breast. Malaí laid the little figure on her bed of leaves.

The next day Malaí went to the sand-that-burns-the-feet, right during the height of the day. She carried a pretty container she had decorated herself, full of water-to-drink for Karincai, who was fishing for oysters.

In the afternoon in the village, the old women, their skin hanging in folds of flesh already dry because of the age of their bodies, did their essential work in a circle of conversation. It was very important to separate the fibers of the vegetable-plants that the boys brought from the forest at the water's edge, to stretch the thread of the fibers, forcing them into one continuous piece without a break, and afterwards to coil them onto a piece of bone. Then the young women could use them to join together skins taken from the big-beasts, to wrap up the men and women.

In the afternoon in the village, the young women, with their skin glowing from the heat of the day, mixed their laughter so it seemed to be one, and imitated, with pretty sounds in their throats, the noises of the birds which exchanged calls in the tall-plants. The young women did other work which was vital and required patience. A great deal of persistence was needed to polish the men's tools (which were made of rough stone) until they were completely smooth. They used sand and water, and with a piece of wood kept on scraping and scraping. The sand and the water scraped on the stones and on the ears, penetrating the quiet of the day and seeming to give off extra heat around the women. Their skin glowed even more, until the eye-of-fire from way up high slipped to the other side of the great hill, behind which they knew were many dangerous pathways.

At the end of the afternoon in the village, with the old women and young women finishing their work, Malaí arrived with her container full of water-from-the-stones and Karincai arrived with his net full of closed-shells. They came from opposite sides of the village, and heard from far off the coughing which tore the chests of the old women.

Two big holes hidden with sticks and leaves had already been prepared between the tall-plants at the entrance to the village, so that any wild beasts which wandered around at night would fall in unexpectedly. For instance, there was the great beast whose skin was sometimes white, sometimes yellow, and sometimes had dark-eyes scattered over it. This beast had enormous fangs and horrible claws which could tear a man's skin with just one blow, making-flesh come off and red spurt out, with no way to put it back inside.

Ua, the hunter, finished throwing many leaves over the hidden holes, thinking hard about the fat flesh of the large animal with dark fur and a big head with thick tufts of hair on it, because who knows what a strong thought would end up calling? Who knows if from far away there might come a large wild beast with dark fur and a big head with thick tufts of hair on it, a male responding to the call of the large dark animal with a big head which Ua formed in his thoughts? He thought female, and thought very hard, until the bones beneath his hair hurt. If thoughts formed an image within his head, this image he had made certainly ought to be of some use after he had expended so much thought. That idea formed itself so easily, with no pain in his head. But if he thought very hard it hurt, just as it hurt for the women to make the live-figures of little-people. Who knows if with a very strong thought the head could also split and there might appear the live-figure of a large animal with a big head with thick tufts of hair on it, just as the women did with the little-people?

Ua was one of the few who did not tremble at fangs or claws. He knew the smell, the call, and the signs left along the path by each different wild animal. Ua took to the other side of the shell-mounds the scraps from what the village had already used and left them there to tantalize the throats of the most fierce of the wild animals that frequented the area, attracted there by this custom. And so there were always some animals for the traps. Ua watched over the traps; there was no danger, as long as no people crossed over them!

Sometimes one of the tribe was more daring, crossing over the limits of nature, doing things with strange results or talking against the oldest ones, putting the others of the tribe in danger, or showing cowardice. Sometimes this daring was paid for in a night

with arms and legs imprisoned by thick cords, with the scraps
from what had already been used by the village, on the other side
of the shell-mounds. . . .

Ua wrinkled his forehead and crumpled up his face, crushing
an uncomfortable idea: When could people think things out of the
ordinary thoughts of everybody, or do what was different, without
having to pay for it with cords and wild animals? Ua, like Karincai, was descended in a long ling from the hill-people. Although
they were like sons of the tribe, they carried in their ideas some
incompatible differences.

At nightfall in the village, when the old women and young
women were completing their tasks, Ua came in with his work
finished. He heard from far off the scraping of stone on the
rounded hollow of another stone as the young women struck
flakes to give flame, and heard from far off the scraping of roots
in bowls as the old women ground meal.

Ua was the only hunter-young-man in the village. There were
many, many other young men who went out with their poles with
sharpened points or with their nets woven of fastened threads,
searching for fish in the angry-waters, and many others who were
taught to dive to collect shells.

Ua, who had a great shock of dark hair and hard, strong undu-
lations of flesh on his arms and chest, stretched out his big body
on the trampled ground of the hut. He made a great "AH" with his
open mouth, calling sleep. High on the shell-mounds, a little
beyond the village, the total darkness was cut by tongues of live-
fire from the enormous hearth built of stones, which was fed by
the women with dried parts of plants. The reddish tongues
climbed up into the darkness with their own sounds. There were
the noises of the flames and the noises of the night. The women
threw the shells into the fire without paying attention to the
sounds of the night. But Ua paid attention. His ear glued to the
smooth ground, Ua classified the sounds made by the big animals
trailing through the forest, and by the smaller ones, and the dis-
agreeable noise of the little beasts which flew at night through the
hut, persistently trying to drink the blood of the young man.

When the tongues-of-fire held themselves up, the women went
into their huts in the village. The men went up onto the shell-
mound in groups and squatted down all around the steaming
shells. While they devoured oysters and mussels with the power
of their teeth and the persistence of their stomachs, they threw the

shells behind their heads, onto the mound of other shells, honoring their valiant chiefs who for many, many ages had been buried there beneath them.

The Council of Old Men was meeting.

It was the night when Malaí came in with her bowl full of water-from-the-stones, when Karincai came in with his net full of closed-shells, the same night when Ua came into the village with his trap ready to ensnare big wild animals, that the Council of Old Men met to decide what to do with the new gift of the Companion-Spirit.

Earlier that same day Malaí's hair had again run around her head, looking like a newly escaped devil. The sand had run around itself and, after rising to the height of a big man, had suddenly traveled in walls of grains, as though they were minuscule furious animals which flew in swarms and attacked Karincai and Malaí. Small roots of green-plants jumped up from the sand-earth. Far away the water had a dark color. Huge sections of water lifted up and drove through the large black mass which hid the blue (the sky might be overhead). The dark angry-waters seemed to want to eat the sand; the sand seemed to want to eat the green-plants. Karincai surrounded Malaí with his entire length, and sought, without seeing with his eyes, the entrance to the cave. He held in his head an image of the place, reproduced from his many visits there. Fighting against the grains which flew all around aimlessly, he managed to lead her there accurately, by felicitous chance. Stumbling in, they fell to the ground exhausted.

A frail light crept along the walls of the cave. Karincai realized that when it had traveled a short space-time, everything would become dark. Outside, the weight of nature descended, all made of water and successive bursts of immense noises. Everything must be opening up in pieces; it seemed that nothing would survive!

Malaí trembled, fearful of passing the whole long dark-time here, far from the village and the protection of the others, in this hole which might be inhabited by wild animals!

Karincai talked about safety, and tried hard to believe in himself. The light moved farther along the wall and Malaí's face was left entirely in shadow. That was when the long hairy legs of a beast scraped Malaí's arm (a scream!), climbing up over her shoulder. Karincai banged a stone with precision and accuracy, and the beast wrapped its enormous legs around its small round body (it was almost the size of a hand, and hairy). Malaí sobbed in horrified shock as the light reached almost to the end of the wall. The wings of beasts which cling to the skin to suck out the body's insides were strewn over the ceiling (they slept hanging). Malaí was all fear. Noises came from all corners of her imagination through the walls. Not even the enormous noises outside, of plants being uprooted and stripped, of rocks crashing off other rocks, of great flashes of fire in the black sky, and of thundering, hid from her ears the little noises of the scraping and clinging lives of the small beasts, their shells and wings in the holes of the night. Malaí waited at every moment for them to walk on her body and bite her flesh.

Karincai covered Malaí's tiny, trembling body with his own large body; when there was no more light on the walls, they rolled up together and waited.

When the light entered the mouth of the cave again and awoke Karincai, who was tangled in Malaí's hair, they went outside where the world seemed to have been put in its place again, and there was no more power which shook up things. They saw Kaúma arrive in a trunk-that-floats from the angry-waters, which were again calm.

Kaúma was the one who opened the bodies of big-plants with live-flames, making long holes inside to produce trunks-that-float. He and many others went into the angry-water inside them, spearing fish. They went this way from one land to another farther ahead on the waters, and threw out their nets to bring back food.

Kaúma arrived with a voice full of harsh cries, and with arms flailing. He wanted to shout what had happened, but it was from a distance so great that no one could understand anything.

When Kaúma came near he managed to make them hear. "It was magic," said Kaúma, "the greatest happening of all, there in the other land. A short distance away in the waters by the trunk-that-floats"—Kaúma turned around to point—"an enormous beast was carried by the terrible night of evil-spirits. It was guided, certainly, by the Companion-Spirit, for there is no evil without good!"

A great-blue-animal, which comes from the depths of the angry-water, was smashed against the far-off rocks. A little distance away by the trunk-that-floats (Kaúma had gestured), it was imprisoned in the rocks. It was immense, with meat enough for a long, long time, and thick skin, and fat inside, and bones to make implements of defense for men. It was enormous!

"Let Kaúma tell in the village of the great present from the spirits," he said.

Kaúma knew, and Karincai and Malaí and everybody knew, what it meant for the shell-mound people to have a big-blue-animal, with thick skin and fat inside, caught between the rocks: a long, long time of plenty. It was a sign of peace from the Companion-Spirit, who gives so much only when he has good will.

A big-blue-animal, almost stone in the light of day (only it could not be stone because its shiny top rose and fell), could be seen once the trunks-that-float came near with their centers full of men, as many as could fit without sinking.

A big-blue-animal like this, which for many was only a story, had begun their village, it was said.

One day a great rage of waters and skies mixed together had made a big-blue-animal misjudge distances. It had thick skin and a mouth full of crisscrossed teeth. That day the men and women had a great deal of meat to eat, and many hard parts to use for implements of defense. They had begun in this exact place a shell-mound (the place, they said, shown by magic), and established a village nearby. Much time had passed, and many events. Men had come from women, grown their bodies, and begun to shrink. Men ended within their bodies, and the bravest and the chiefs were buried in the middle of the shells with everything that was theirs (things, conquered enemies, women). Men came from high up in far-off lands, and fought; many died, but the small children and women stayed. They brought new and different ideas, and taught the old villagers. New men were born of women, and it all happened again. It was as they said it had been, and one day it would happen again.

The Council of Old Men meeting that night on the shell-mound decided who would go and who would stay. First only the men would go, for the initial work. Then the women would go with the children. The old people and the weak ones would stay.

Many utensils of smoothed stone shaped into points and many sharpened-sticks were carried by the chosen strong men, who were led by Ua the hunter.

Now, cutting through the angry-waters in trunks-that-float, the men came closer and closer to the great rock which was becoming, increasingly, the storied great-blue-animal.

The eye-of-fire suddenly rolled up overhead like a ball. Karincai collected it all in his eyes. He could not tolerate the eye-of-fire, which he had an obsession to look at, to try to see the form behind the flames. While he pushed away the angry-waters with a stick flattened on one end (they all did this, to propel the trunk-that-floats), Karincai directed crazy thoughts toward the eye-of-fire, faced it, collected it all in his eyes, and could not tolerate it. He captured a view of shining sand inside his eyes, and the eye-of-fire remained an image made on the dark of Karincai's eyes. What could be that thing which moved regularly with each lightness and went away each time of darkness?

On the beach at the village, becoming smaller and smaller there, far from his eyes, Malaí received on her face the same light-warmth. She did not think anything; she only felt. Malaí had a nature made only to feel things.

Chapter 2

The world of the other side. The beast with the hooked face. The marks that mean each thing. Of how shock-terror entered the lives of men. Of how Manaú went to live with the shell-spirits.

The place was a huge world of white-sand, which would not fit within a single glance. The hollow-trunks stopped there, and the men got out to follow one another's footsteps on the whiteness. It was so fluffy that they left no marks as they passed along the ground.

It appeared that there had never been any humans in this place, because when they passed, the beasts flew away suddenly in the first shock of their lives. From time to time, retreating ponderously in their immense shells, enormous green-animals with hooked faces abandoned the white-sands where they had spent the night, to return to the angry-waters in which they dwelled. The men knew about the tasty meat of the hooked-face animal, the round, slow burden of four little feet. The men ran to surround and capture one. Ua brandished in his strong hands a smoothed stone with two sharp-pointed sides. The men secured the big ani-

mal and turned it over by its little feet. It lay with its stomach up
and its scarred green shell below, pulling its head and extremities
into its shell. The men did not worry; they knew it could not flee
this way. They would return later when the immense heat of the
day tormented the animal, so that it freed its feet and put out its
head, straining and straining to turn back over. The men would
cut off its unusable feet and head with their tools, and let the
blood run out of the animal by leaning it up for a while.

While the great green hooked-face animal which fortune had
already designated for them remained overturned, the men went
to look on the sands, because they knew why the round-beast had
come. Many times during the night it had laid a large number
(many times the fingers on a hand) of eggs in a hole made in the
sand, which it covered up again afterwards. Then it had returned
to the angry-waters, leaving it to the eye-of-fire to awaken life
within the little eggs. It would return from time to time (perhaps
two or three times) to fill the same hole with new eggs. The
beasts did that only in new sand where (woe to them!) men had
not walked even once. There was no more terrible wild animal
known to the others than the big animal-man, who had ideas in
his thinking head.

Kaúma and another man, Manaú, who always joined him for
the heaviest work, turned over the sands to see where the shelled-
beast might have carried itself during the night. Finally they
found a suspicious-looking place and dug around it until they
found the eggs. There were so many that the men, who liked them
very much, filled a net bag up to the brim. Still more eggs remained. Since men are not animals which leave behind extra
food, they brought back another empty net to fill.

Manaú and Kaúma said to one another, "What a wonderful
place for a new shell-mound, with the huts over there," and "It's
too bad the beasts-that-fly left here in surprise."

Many other men joined them. After they had eaten a few eggs
(each one made a hole in a shell and sucked out the insides
through that hole with his mouth), they surrounded with tools and
curiosity the great-blue-animal, which was a rock in the morning.

Ua used his great strength to open a hole in the thick skin on
top of the big-blue-animal, until the blubber inside could be seen.
The other men separated the skin from the blubber beneath it. The
heat growing in the day was making colors shimmer. The skin of
the beast came off thick and blue, the yellowish red skin of the

men was shining wet, the blubber was white, the eye-of-fire up above was yellow, the angry-water down below was blue, and the sand which would not fit completely within one glance was white.

The men chased a hooked-face animal for a long time, even in the water. They had devised a very clever method for doing this. They caught some fish which had along their bodies strange parts which fastened on things. The men tied these fish to their rods, and with them chased the animal. The strange-fish held on to the shell of the hooked-face beast so strongly that the men could pull without fear that one would come loose from the other.

Men, without fangs or claws, and with thin skin on their flesh, found ways to conquer other animals. Almost always.

The thick blue skin of the big animal gradually dried on stakes fastened in the white-sand. The day began to cast shadows.

The men turned their feet toward the trunks-that-float. They slowly dragged along the hooked-face beast with its feet torn off. It no longer moved, but dripped blood on the sand. The men still carried many eggs in the net bag. They came tired, the sky dripping blood up high, the great darkness peeping through in the shadow on each rock, the darkness growing.

Huge shadows all around became ever darker until their edges joined in the darkness of one great shadow.

On the village beach, which was getting bigger, Malaí felt the gentle-breath on her face. Far off on the floating-trunks a figure grew in her eyes; it was Karincai arriving. The hollow-trunks became larger and larger. There were no longer images, only noise, when the men dragged them up onto the sand. Malaí felt the taste of salt on Karincai's chest, but her eyes no longer saw anything. A line of torches came down the beach, lighting up the hands and faces of a band of men.

The men carried on their shoulders the big meaty and dismembered shell of the green-animal with the hooked face. With the torches in front opening up the darkness, they went along the path shouting to chase away unfriendly spirits.

At the entrance to the village many women, children with faces full of questions and astonished eyes which were lit up like torches, and old men made a path so the young men could carry in their prey and tools, which exhaustion made heavier.

Enormous tongues-of-fire from the stone hearths burned a piece of the darkness and sent warm smoke around the heads of the old men sitting there in consultation. The young fishermen, Kaúma and Manaú, Ua and the others, were already stretched out in their huts, feeling the tiredness in their arms and legs.

Malaí threw a gourd of water onto Karincai's chest, and then she rubbed on him some leaves, which she knew produced a smell to keep away the little animals which suck the skin.

The next day the men would go back in their trunks-that-float, a space-time from the village on the angry-waters, to the magic place for a new shell-mound.

The big eye-of-fire already floated on the waters of the morning.

The big eye-of-fire sometimes floats on the angry-waters and sinks, but still, it seems, it never goes out. In addition, the yellow sometimes turns red, and it grows and shrinks a little, depending on whether it is more or less hot. Karincai paid attention to those differences.

Karincai also noticed that the breath-that-moves-things has a certain time and always lasts the same space. It comes from the angry-water to breathe on the village, and it comes from the village to breathe on the angry-water. Karincai created a symbol in his head, choosing a figure of thought to say "each breath in its own time." He also thought of some images to say "the eye-of-fire" and "the white-eye of night," and marked them all down in the sand. But the breath-of-air became stronger and the angry-water came up, lapping the beach and undoing everything.

The next day the angry-water went back down, erasing the marks on the wet sand. Karincai then thought that the angry-water has a time when it grows and takes up more beach, and a time when it goes back down; it was not always the same size. Karincai ached from such thoughts. Since he did not have anyone to entrust with his insights, he thought of marks to record the things in his memory. Because the sand soon lost any signs made on it, one day he went way back into the cave. He drew on the walls, with his sharpened tool for opening shells, the symbols which stood for each thing. He marked down the breath-of-air, the angry-water, the eye-of-fire, and the white-eye. He represented Malaí with a rounded design which he liked to draw, and he repeated it many times. He also portrayed the big-blue-animal and the green-animal with the hooked face, whose shell the women split down the middle so they could take out the meat and make use of the shell.

He made many marks, which became each thing for him. He drew on an entire wall of the cave. Afterwards he went out noiselessly, guarding his secret, for no one knew of the place except Malaí.

After they fed the men hot broth made of pounded meat, the women carried their tools through the sands to the trunks, for a new day was passing through the sky with the moving eye.

The men entered the bellies of the trunks, which sighed because they were so full, and pushed with the sticks-flattened-on-the-end so that the sand remained behind. The trunks cut through the waters for a space-time to the great white beach where the sands-without-end disappeared under the great-blue-animal, which looked almost like a rock in the morning. From afar they saw many animals flying, circling overhead. When the men arrived, the beasts-that-fly took their flight a greater distance away.

Once the trunks were taken care of, the men went on their way before the day could put the heat of fire on the white-ground, even close to the wetness. When they came nearer to the almost-rock, which was the animal against the white-blue of the morning, they stopped short. They halted, each one seeing the horror of his own eyes reflected in the eyes of the others.

At first the words were caught in their throats and could not come out. Afterwards they made only sounds, as though everyone were afraid, afraid of saying to one another what they all knew was passing through the awareness of each one.

The closer they came, the more their eyes saw, not believing, but seeing. There was the big-blue-animal, with its skin almost entirely taken off by all their work the previous day. Enormous holes had been dug into the blubber, and the meat had been devoured, in some places all the way to the bones. That was why the little animals were flying around overhead so much, because it was easy to bite off mouthfuls. The dark red, naked meat laughed through the holes, like the gums of old men! It seemed impossible that during the space of just one dark-time the beasts-that-fly had managed to devour so much in such a horrible manner.

There existed only one animal capable of doing this, and that was the horror. The fear in the eyes of everybody was imprinted in the eyes of each one; the image of the same animal was constructed at the same time in all their heads. It was of an animal which was also blue, but one the men wanted to see only from a greater distance. From time to time, however, a braver man stabbed such an enormous fish with his stick-with-sharpened-point, as a trophy for his bravery. It was as big as two men end to end, and had an enormous mouth full of successive rows of teeth, terrible teeth capable of cutting anything, be it animal or man. From time to time one was stranded in the shallow-water. It did not allow itself to be caught in woven nets; it tore everything, and knocked over the trunks with a blow of its tail. All wild animals seemed to lose a little of their fierceness when put side by side with this one in the memory, image against image.

Once a fierce-blue-animal was dead, its skin was of the best quality. Its teeth could be useful in many possible ways. Fastened together along the length of a piece of wood, they could be used to saw things. Singly, fastened onto points of sticks, they were used to stab fish and little animals. And fastened together on a fiber thread, after holes were laboriously made in them, they made ornaments which were very pretty to look at, and which everyone wanted to wear, because things are worth more when there are only a few of them and they are difficult to find.

The men knew, as they looked sadly at the cut-up animal, that only many ferocious-blue-fish all together could produce this result. The men had to be very careful now wading through those angry-waters, sending ahead their apprehensions and much caution.

With vigorous strokes of the tools in their hands they cut the remaining meat, forming heaps on the sand. They went around the animal carefully, suspicious of the slightest movement of the waters. The men worked for a long time without stopping. The meat, a very dark red, formed mounds on the sand; now only bones shaped in a large curve were left. Within that arch, unexpectedly, uncountable little fish and other beasts still jumped in the shallow-water that entered the carcass. Manaú stood in it up to his knees. There were so many little fish, and they jumped! The men laughed at the little beasts, which had probably been the blue-animal's last meal. There were so many, they looked like little beasts-that-fly in the unsettled shallow-waters, and they looked as if they were alive. Manaú used his hands to grab the fish as they jumped. All the men forgot their fears, laughing.

Manaú walked on the body of the animal, inside the curved-white-bones, water up to his knees, walking, laughing. . . .

Suddenly there was a roar. Manaú was dragged down by a leg. His two arms were flailing and grabbing on to the great-bone of the meatless animal, and the other men were dizzy with incomprehension. In a nothing of time Kaúma saw a dark point leaving the shallow angry-water and the water turning red around them. Manaú was shouting more loudly. Kaúma went into the water quickly and with all his strength pulled Manaú up by the arms. The others helped, everybody already understanding. They lifted Manaú's body, which was trembling at the mouth and everywhere else. Finally they lifted up a horrible lacerated stump of a leg, red from flesh torn off a little below the knee.

The men encircled Manaú in silence. Each one became a small part of Manaú in his sharp pain. Each one lost a little of the red from within his own body through Manaú's leg. This could soon be seen in their faces, which were white with shock.

Many strong men lifted Manaú and put him, dripping blood, on their shoulders, as they had done the day before with the green-animal with the hooked face. They made their footsteps go through the white-sands, returning silently to the trunks-that-float. They placed Manaú in the bottom of a hollow-trunk. Using their sticks-that-move-water, they went through the angry-water to the beach at the village, where no one was waiting.

Taking the body from the trunk-that-floats, the men went on up to the village, carrying that sad load on their shoulders.

The girl-woman pushed each long-thin stick into a hole in the ground where a good-plant would grow, so it could climb up the stick to overcome the bad-plants. Good-plants had long-rounded roots and yellow-rounded ones, which the women prepared as food.

When the girl-woman turned her head and collected the rest of the light in her eyes to measure the life of the darkness for enough time to drive in many other sticks, she grasped with a half-gesture at a noise in the air.

She stopped.

The almost shapeless long smooth body of the girl-woman stopped to listen. Then she straightened her trunk, bent her legs, and ran into the village with a warning, stretching her legs as far as they could reach.

Old men formed walls with boy-men, young women and old ones, and children made holes in this wall with the sharpness of their eyes. They all questioned her:

"Girl-woman said?"

"That she heard the noise of men coming, whoever they were or were not. . . ."

"Girl-woman heard?"

"When she made holes in the earth with wood-stakes so the good-plants could grow, she heard . . ."

". . . girl-woman heard, and did not have courage to stay to see, but came running in a hurry to warn the village!"

The women spoke many words, all mixed up with the others; no one heard anyone, not even their own words, which were lost in the mixture. Men exchanged big, wide gestures; no one paid attention to the gestures of another, and lost their own in the mixture of all. Men and women lost their gestures and their words in one great noise and motion, and could not extract any sense from it.

In the chaos of their own confusion they were careless about the arrival of the young men, who came into the village almost without being sensed. Thus the men carried in their burden and put down Manaú, who had no further awareness of pain or life. Gestures and words stopped as though cut off, and a heavy silence descended like a trap over all the lowered heads.

Mamazu, an old man whose age the fingers of many hands could not count, took a step which broke through the wall of squeezed-together people, came to the front, and gave orders. Mamazu controlled the use of magic, and talked with the spirits, both the good and the evil-companions. He gave orders to carry Manaú to the highest shell-mound. They all went, each one behind the feet of another. Manaú's woman-companion sobbed lament-shrieks, ground her teeth together, and twisted her face into the most horrible expressions.

"If only Manaú could live! . . ."

She knew that she belonged to Manaú, to follow him in life or death.

While everyone stood at the top of the shell-mound, Mamazu tightly tied fibers around Manaú's middle-leg, until the red which was soaking the fibers stopped running. Manaú did not awaken to life. Mamazu prepared some magic words and ordered Kaúma to find a strong branch from a wood-plant and make a whole perfect leg, in imitation of Manaú's leg when it was good.

Kaúma found a strong wood-plant, took off the bark with a tongue-of-flame, and prepared the shape of a leg just like Manaú's when it was good. After the leg was made Mamazu took it, put it on top of Manaú's half-leg, and said:

"Now his leg is whole, good for much walking and strong like this wood-plant."

Manaú could not use the strong-magic of a new leg, because his spirit had gone to live with the companion-spirits inside a shell.

Women and children went back down to the village. The men stayed, saying magic words around Manaú, and piling many spirit-shells around his head, so that the I-living of Manaú could leave him completely and enter the shells. Of the women, only Manaú's companion remained. She lay down beside him. She waited quietly, with no more shouts or laments, for her I-living to pass to the shells along with that of her companion.

Men went down to search for all of Manaú's things, big and little, and took them all back up to their owner. They recited a list of Manaú's things:

Two gourds to collect sweet-water and food-plants; a big net made of knotted fiber-threads, for catching fish; two sharpened-stakes to spear bigger fish in shallow-waters; very fine bones with holes in one end, for his woman-companion to use to fasten to-gether animal skins; fine bones without holes in the ends, to make holes in teeth or stones; a circle with a hole bored in the middle, to wind plant-fibers; big stones very cleverly smoothed into shapes with two points, for opening large fruits and roots and for tearing apart meat; precious teeth from the great ferocious animal with yellow spots and big fangs and claws and many agile and dangerous jumps; a large number of beautiful round-bones from the backs of fish, very attractively identical and strung on threads; and other precious ornaments.

The men very respectfully put Manaú's belongings around his body. Then they surrounded everything with rough rocks to sepa-rate it from the remaining space.

The old men said that because Manaú had used his own hands to tear off the legs of the green-animal which he himself had found, the blue-animal had taken revenge by tearing off his leg. Just as the green-animal had his end, so Manaú would have the same end. Manaú should have let an uninvolved man from the village, who had not participated in capturing the animal and was innocent of that, cut up the pieces. These things ought to be done just as they had to be, so not to awaken the vengeance of the evil-spirits.

The darkness climbed up the shell-mound and stretched out to the village, but the men did not return to their huts. Instead, they searched nearby for piles of earth colored with red-paint. They rubbed the red-grains with their fingers to dry the dampness from it in the heat of the big hearth. They kept rubbing it and drying the dampness from the paint even more. The fingers of the men became very red from rubbing the grains. Finally Mamazu thought it was ready, and ordered them to use it to cover Manaú's entire body. This was done to replace the color which Manaú had lost, to guarantee other-life. Since no one here could live without red-color, it was appropriate to provide it for the other life. Similarly, they furnished food and objects so Manaú could go beyond with his companion, his belongings, and everything he needed. They sprinkled red-paint over the entire body of Manaú and of his woman-companion, who was now motionless like a dead-body.

When they had fed the great fire and piled up shells, they ate some and covered Manaú's body with other whole ones. The I-living of Manaú was no longer him, but was now only what remained inside the shells which the old men, very considerately, had used to surround his head after they had taken a little of that spirit in the oysters which they swallowed. The woman-companion of Manaú let herself be buried with him. Her eyes were turned toward the darkness inside, and she was already convinced she was no longer alive in her body. The old men and the young ones spent the night eating the insides of shells and piling other whole ones on Manaú, his companion, and his belongings.

The most magic, much-awaited, and important moment arrived. Manaú had been a very beloved fisherman with strong arms. The strength of Manaú's arms was in his flesh, not in his I-living. The men wanted to save within themselves, within their bodies, in homage and compassion, and also for their own benefit, the good-strength in Manaú's arms. Some young fishermen and Ua the hunter were chosen by the Council of Old Men for this cherished ceremony.

The tongues-of-fire climbed up the sides of the darkness with greater strength and heat. Manaú's woman-companion suffocated beneath the great number of shells that had fallen on top of her. The legs of Manaú's body were bent up to this stomach, preparing him for a good long sleep. His spirit had already gone to live in the hard shells of the soft animal-spirits. There remained only the strength which his arms retained.

The men took up their weapons next to Manaú's body. They held his arms out and cut them off at the shoulders. Then they cooked his flesh, and ate the strength of Manaú which resided in his arms, with all the gratitude and respect that this important and thoughtful act required.

Chapter 3

The terrible secret-place where no woman walks. The spirit which swallows boys and returns men. A certain Camiú, who they say talks with the wild animals, who they say bewitches people, and other magic. Karincai's secret. On how men punish. The evil which became good.

Malaí crossed over the paths of many still-waters, treacherous eyes-of-darkness with sand underneath and depths that become deeper within themselves, so that no one knows where they end. They were sleeping warm pools of water, with the day above repeated in them. Woe to anyone who fell in! There were others in which you could submerge your body and cross to the other side without danger. Karincai knew which ones were waters-for-submerging and which were treacherous-waters.

Malaí walked between the green-plants on the path. Little beasts were running across her eyes, life moving through the forest.

A surprised little beast cut in front of Malaí, climbed up a plant, and clung to the trunk with sharp claws. It jumped from one plant to another through the space above, and then dug itself into the dark loose mud on the edge of the waters. Another little animal, with many spikes all over its body, passed by farther off. They say that brave men do not eat the good-flesh of the little spiked-animal because it rolls itself up with fear, and this cowardly-fright would become part of anyone who ate its flesh!

Malaí traveled across the paths. On the murky edges of a big-water she barely saw two bulging eyes and two tunnel-caverns on the end of a big-muzzle (which hid an enormous mouth full of saw-teeth), moving in the depths of the water.

Malaí moved back to a path farther in the forest. Walking on, she met Ua, who was preparing a trap especially for the terrible long-beast of the muddy-water. These beasts, which stayed hidden below the water, had skin made of pieces of different forms and sizes fastened together.

Malaí pointed out where the bulging-eyes disturbed the big-water.

Ua inserted his pointed-stick, which had two sharpened ends, into the dead-body of a little furry-animal which had lived at the edge-of-the-water. He fastened it sturdily onto a tip of the stick with a fiber from a tree, and secured the other side of the stick to a tree trunk. Afterwards he threw the little animal to the edge of the muddy big-water, where there was movement, and he waited.

Leaving Ua, Malaí continued walking to where the greenery turned the day darker. She walked; for a long time she walked. Suddenly tiredness put dryness into her mouth. Then Malaí heard the noise of water nearby, and she went a little off the usual path. The green-color there was softened by increased humidity, which she knew indicated the proximity of water-to-drink.

Malaí pushed away the vegetation and went down into the underbrush. The noise was more obvious there, becoming louder and louder. suddenly it was real, happy dancing water, clear, without color, and full of motion!

Happy-waters jumped between the great rocks, and gave off colors in the air on their journey.

Malaí ran, laughing; her two hands were the two sides of an opened shell. When she came close her face interrupted the smile of the happy-water as it tumbled. The water ran down Malaí's hair—how good it felt! It was only then that she became aware of the place.

Malaí stopped in astonishment.

She knew about this place; she had heard it described many

times in the village. Beyond, the wooden shelter jumped out at her from the amazing stories she had heard. Suddenly it was there in the middle, the great hut half hidden in the greenery, in a mute and closed silence. It was the silence of emptiness. It was empty because no one ever came near there, except once in each complete-time, when Mamazu brought the boy-men for the great dangerous journey from which they would return as young men.

They said in the village (Malaí had heard the stories they told) that a strong-spirit lived there, a terrible-spirit which swallowed boy-men and gave back young men. No woman could step near this place, and none had ever seen it.

Malaí trembled, looking to all sides, which were all empty, wondering where the strong-spirit, who put such fear in the mother-women, stayed.

Did the terrible-spirit always stay, perhaps, locked in the hut?

The silence became more intense all around. No life was apparent here, nor, it seemed, did plants move. Malaí wanted to return her feet to the path, but she was glued there by the tales she had heard. No woman had ever been there, certainly!

The tales said that the red-cords which unite little children to the bodies of their mothers were deposited in this water. They said they threw them in a pool of deep water so the little children would grow up without fear of going into the water and would become good fishermen! They said it was the second-soul-twin of the first child, which was not born but became an important protecting soul for the first-born. When Ua was born, his red-cord, he said, was hung on a very high tree in the half-darkness of the forest. Instead of a fisherman, then, the second-brother-soul of Ua made him a valiant hunter, without fear of wild animals, fangs, or claws. The red-cord of Malaí had been planted in the earth so that she could learn with her second-sister-soul to work with food-plants.

Suddenly Malaí's whole body shook with cold-fear—what if someone saw the young woman there? She looked again toward the quiet hut and thought it was very quiet indeed. Perhaps the terrible-spirit was sleeping.

"Who knows, maybe he only wakes up in time to swallow boy-men, and afterwards, tired from such a great feat, sleeps for a long time?"

Malaí shook the water from her hair and sought to return to the old path. She was now, suddenly, in a great hurry. She hastened to

flee from the strange-quiet place before any terrible-spirit should
discover her or old man go past her, for only old men may talk
with such difficult spirits.

While Malaí walked along the trail little colored-beasts beat
their wings in the path of her eyes. Others made a buzzing noise
at the entrance to her ears. And there were other beautiful things.

Malaí was going that long distance to see an old man called
Camiú, an old man so old that his voice had dried in his throat,
like the flesh beneath his skin. Camiú spent the light-time of day
working with green-plants, moving them, taking new ones and
growing adults, and making with them, they said, magic which
was only his own.

The old man without a voice in his mouth dug his curved
fingers into the earth and moved it and pulled at roots and put in
plants. Then a finished plant with green husks and red hair on the
point on top was born. He took off the husks; inside them were
long-rounded forms which had yellow-grains fastened to them.
No one knew what they were for. He took the grains from the
long-rounded forms, filled a gourd with them, and saved them.
Sometimes an animal came during the night and stole them. The
old man screamed without-sound, waving his raised arms. He
scarcely had enough energy, and dragged along like a beast himself. No one knew what the yellow-grains were, nor what they
were for, because he could not respond to anything he was asked.

Camiú was a frail old man who neither hunted nor fished. He
lived outside the village. He ate, they said, magically, because he
planted weird plants which no one knew how to eat. The wild
beasts did not touch him, and it was said that because he was a
mute-speaker, he understood their eyes.

One day Camiú saw Malaí and smiled in a friendly way. Malaí
came up curiously to study the old man. Camiú liked Malaí and
gave her a plant as a present. He taught her to mash it with her
fingers and mix it in water. At first Malaí was suspicious, but
afterwards she took the gourd in her hands and drank. After a
short time Malaí felt a smile free itself from her mouth in great
happiness, and she laughed, and laughed, and laughed, and the
old man laughed without-sound at Malaí's happiness, and the two
laughed, and laughed, and laughed. Camiú liked Malaí and gave
her a small piece of the plant-that-laughs for her to take with her.
Camiú also gave Malaí the plant she had rubbed on Karincai's

body, with the strong smell to chase away the little beasts which drink through the skin.

That day Malaí had taken a piece of the herb-that-laughs with her to the beach, where she met Karincai. The dark-body that accompanied Malaí, lying down and dragging along the ground, had stretched out long, which meant that the eye-of-fire was going away and it was the end of the day. At the height of the day the dark-body almost disappears beneath the body. Afterwards, the more the day passes, the more the dark-body becomes long-skinny and grows larger. By measuring its size, Malaí knew what part of the day it was.

While she walked along the beach, followed by her long dark-body, Malaí saw Karincai from afar. He came out of the angry-water and ran fleeing from an enormous blue-wall of water, which rose behind his back and tried to swallow the young man. He was running, but the blue-wall, taller-faster, reached Karincai's body and hit him with a loud noise. It seemed that it would knock him over, but no, the great-water slid off Karincai's strong trunk and descended smoothly, turning foamy white and dressing the young man's body. Malaí thought it was lovely, and ran to meet Karincai, who wore white foam-lace. They rolled together, a living wave, through the white-blue up to the sand.

The eye-of-fire at the edge of the sky came to dry the white foam gradually from the body of Malaí–Karincai. The body of Malaí–Karincai did not even feel the eye-of-fire, because inside it there rose a blue-wave which swallowed the outside world.

Karincai led Malaí by the hand to see the cave, because, he said, he had a secret to show her. Malaí, very curious, ran to keep up with Karincai's big-wide steps. Malaí's hair, hanging behind her, flew as she ran. Following Malaí and Karincai came the dark-bodies, dragging along the ground, Malaí's running, and Karincai's with big-wide steps.

When they reached the mouth of the cave, Karincai led Malaí deep inside to see a big wall full of drawing-designs. Malaí stopped in front of it and stared, astonished. Karincai stood look-ing at Malaí's amazed face. He was laughing a great deal, very happily. Karincai's breast, and Malaí's, were heaving inside and out with the tiredness of running. Karincai was laughing, and Malaí was astonished.

"What is it?"

Karincai came close to the marked wall. Pointing with his finger, he showed her the rounded drawing which appeared many times, saying, "This is Malaí."

Malaí looked at Karincai with even more shocked astonishment. Karincai continued showing signs to her, saying, "This is the yellow-eye of day, this is the white-eye of night." Malaí's mouth was open in amazement. Karincai showed her: "This is the green-animal with the hooked face, this is the blue-animal with thick skin, this is the angry-water, this is the sweet-water from the rocks."

Malaí sat down on the floor of the cave, staring open-eyed. She understood; Karincai had invented mark-signs to stand for different things. Crazy Karincai. The Council of Old Men was going to spear Karincai as though he were a fish lost in the shallow-water. Karincai did seem to be a fish lost in the shallow-water of the village men. He had very crazy ideas, different from those of everybody.

Malaí was afraid for Karincai. She looked at Karincai, who laughed. Malaí then felt the drawings mix together and become wet. The water that mixed together the drawings in Malaí's eyes began to run down her face. Malaí's chest made a crazy sound. Karincai stopped laughing. The water rolled down Malaí's face. Karincai touched his fingertips to her face and licked his wet fingers. He found that the water from Malaí's face was salty, and wet his fingers again and licked them. He thought it was good, and drank all the water from her face.

"Why does Malaí spill salty water from her eyes?" (It tasted good; he moved his tongue along the sides of his mouth.) "Is it because of Karincai's drawings on the wall?"

Malaí did not answer. She did not know how to answer. She was just afraid. Very afraid. Afraid for Karincai, not for herself.

Malaí told Karincai not to say anything, not to show the mark-signs on the wall to anyone, ever, nor to tell what they meant to him, that they said things.

Karincai promised not to, but he wanted her to learn what the marks said. Later they would be able to converse with mute-signs, without making a sound!

"Isn't it beautiful?"

Malaí dried the rest of the water from her wet face with her hands, and began to repeat the name of each thing when Karincai showed her the sign with his finger, very patiently.

On the ground, forgotten, lay a piece of the plant-that-laughs, which Camiú had given to her.

When Karincai felt a dryness in his mouth, Malaí remembered and brought him the plant-that-laughs. Malaí told him that Camiú, an old man so old that he had no more voice in his throat, had given her the plant; she told him that if it was crushed with water it made a magic drink which made you laugh, and laugh, and laugh. Karincai wanted to try it. Malaí crushed it with her fingers inside a gourd until it formed broth. She put some in Karincai's mouth, and took some herself.

The things that Karincai saw began to turn into two things each, even two Malaís. Karincai wanted to hold on to Malaí, but went the wrong direction. He thought that everything was very funny, and that Malaí was funny, and he began to laugh. Malaí saw Karincai lift up his body and walk wrong, laughing a great deal, and it was very funny. Karincai's voice became loud-long, like inside a hollow-head; the voice of Karincai came lo-o-o-o-ong to Malaí's ear, and Malaí's ear was hollow. Malaí was a hollow-head, and it was very funny to make it laugh, and laugh, and laugh. She laughed so much that a lot of water squeezed out of her eyes, and it ran out making things wet. Things were different, and not the same anymore. Karincai touched Malaí with his hand. Karincai's hand was hu-u-u-uge, and Malaí's arm seemed thi-i-i-in. They laughed until it hurt the middle of their bodies, which they doubled up without wanting to, and they laughed, and they laughed.

Malaí and Karincai went out through the entrance to their hut, laughing to see colors that had other colors and seemed to be separate from things. The green was green itself, and not just part of the plants. Ua, who was coming near, had a face that he had never had before. Malaí showed Ua's face to Karincai while she laughed, and laughed, and laughed. Karincai laughed and laughed. Ua became very angry and came at Karincai with his big hand closed at the fingers; he shook his fist, but Karincai laughed, and laughed, and laughed. Ua was more annoyed, and pushed hard against Karincai's chest with his big closed hand, so that Karincai fell back onto the ground. It hurt, but he laughed and laughed. Ua thought it was witchcraft, and ran off to find Mamazu.

Women came to find Malaí. Malaí called the women into the

hut and gave them the drink she had made, so they could all try it.
A girl called Ima, who had long hair which greatly pleased Ua,
was the first to drink. After the young women drank, the old
women passed the gourd from hand to hand and mouth to mouth.
Each woman drank and passed it to the others. Ima went out of
the hut laughing at the tickles which went through her throat, and
laughed more and more until more tickles rose in her throat, and
she laughed, and laughed, and laughed. . . .

When the women returned from Malaí and Karincai's hut,
they all laughed a laughter without beginning or end. Mamazu,
arriving with Ua, saw that the laughter was catching from some to
the others. The men came near their women-companions and,
finding them very strange in their ways, became very angry. The
women thought that even funnier, and this made the men angrier.
Some grabbed their women-companions by the hair and dragged
them; the women yelled that it hurt, but laughed. Mamazu
thought, "What terrible magic has attacked all the women of the
village this way?" He tightened the countless lines on his face. Ua
grabbed Ima by her long hair and dunked the girl's face in a big
bowl full of water, making bubbles rise, *blub, blub, blub*. Mamazu pulled hard on Ua's angry hand, which was suffocating
Ima, because anger was not effective against made-magic. It was
necessary to know how the women had received the spell.

The men surrounded Karincai and carried the young man to
the middle of the village. Mamazu spoke to him with great delib-
eration and calm (Karincai had also been attacked by the magic):
"What was the beginning of everything?"

Karincai, laughing a great deal, told him that Malaí had
mashed with her fingers a plant-that-laughs which she had
brought from far away, from a certain Camiú. He was an old man
so old that his voice had already dried up in his throat (some men
knew him), an old man who spent the daylight moving green-
plants and making with them (they said) magic which only he
understood (some had heard). He was an old man without a voice
in his mouth, who had scarcely any strength, who dragged himself along like a beast, an old man who neither fished nor hunted,
who lived outside the village, and who ate (they said) magically,
because he planted weird plants which nobody knew how to eat.

Some men spoke, others told, many knew something, they

had heard said . . . Who else but Camiú could have made such a great spell, produced from a plant?

. . . And the wild beasts do not touch him, and they say that though he cannot speak, he understands their eyes.

Mamazu heard all this, merely shaking his head with his neck, up and down, and from one side to the other.

"What do we have to do?" one of them asked.

"Camiú certainly wants to do away with all the women of the village through some magic means. Who knows, perhaps once he has finished with them, he'll exterminate the whole tribe of our village."

"If there aren't any women, how will there be men afterwards?"

The men spoke. Mamazu thought calmly. The men spoke without stopping.

"Some enemy from another village must have sent—a magic herb he must have sent—which weakens men and makes everybody crazy."

The crazed Karincai did not understand anything in the midst of all the voices and movement. He suddenly had a strong desire to sleep. He rolled himself up right there in his arms and legs, as children sleep, and he slept.

Men carried the sleeping Karincai to the hut. Some worried men tied up their women-companions, for fear they would flee. The women only laughed, and soon began to feel sleepy. Before long they were all asleep.

High on the shell-mound, where tongues-of-fire cut through the darkness, the Council of Old Men met to decide the fate of another old man, Camiú.

Many men accompanied Malaí along the paths of the still-waters, those treacherous eyes-of-darkness which have sand underneath and depths that become deeper and deeper within themselves, so that no one knows where they end. Malaí walked between the green-plants along the pathways, guiding the men. She did not know why, but they wanted to see Camiú. Malaí did not laugh anymore. Little beasts ran across her eyes, their lives moving through the forest.

Malaí kept going in to where the green made the day seem darker. She walked, walked for a long time, with the men behind her. Malaí thought that she liked Camiú, and that Camiú was a good old man. The men had decided that Camiú was bad, and Malaí did not understand: "How could he be-good—be-bad all at the same time?" But the men had decided. Malaí's breast tightened as she walked. She did not know what, but something in the quiet of their voices and the slowness of their movements made her afraid. Malaí hoped: "Let Camiú be far away, don't let him be where he ought to be!"

Malaí went on as small colored-beasts beat their wings in the path of her eyes. Malaí did not see them. Others went *buzz* in the openings of her ears. The men were behind her.

Soon the men saw the old man who dug his curved fingers in the dirt and moved it and pulled out roots and put in plants. The old man without a voice in his mouth, knowing Malaí, laughed in a friendly way. He took some hard yellow-grains from some long-rounded forms, and filled a gourd with them. Malaí stopped where she was; the men continued up to Camiú. The old-old man looked at the men, but could not stand up; he could only drag himself along. The men grabbed Camiú's arms (they were two thin cords), and dragged the living-body of the old man some distance along the ground. The legs of the old man wanted to grab on to the earth, just as the roots do, but the men pulled him hard, and Camiú had no strength. Malaí shut her eyes so she could see no more. The fingers of the old man's feet left a long scratch on the path. He could not scream; the long scratch of the fingers of his feet on the earth, endlessly long, was worth more than a shout. Men grabbed Camiú and carried him to the village.

Some stayed behind to examine the strange plants; they pulled up some and trod on them all. One man kicked over the container of yellow-grains and stepped on them where they fell on the ground, until they all disappeared.

After the men carried Camiú to the village, the sky overturned its gourds and a great deal of water fell right on the trampled ground and the uprooted plants. After this water came, the eye-of-fire returned to float in the blue-space up above. Where the yellow-grains had been stepped on and buried, there poked up a little green-forest and the plants became stronger and bigger. Tall-slim plants with long-thin leaves grew, and in the middle of them, one day, yellow-grains would appear fastened to long-

rounded-white forms, covered with green husks, with red hairs
pointing up.

The young men put Camiú down on the ground in the village.
Mamazu came with the other old men, Tumai among them
(Tumai, who they said knew things about plants), and they took
in their hands the plant-that-laughs which the men had brought.
Tumai smelled the plant-that-laughs, sniffed it, held it tightly with
his fingers, and shook his head from side to side, saying no.
Tumai had never seen this plant; it was strange. It must be a force
for magic and spells.

Mamazu ordered: "Save this plant-that-laughs in your hut, and
examine it later." Now the men had to punish the old man called
Camiú, for trying to cast a spell on the women, and thus destroy
the village by magic.

Camiú, tied up with thick tree-fibers, stayed in a corner, waiting for the two men who had been selected to come and carry the
old-man-without-voice to the farthest shell-mound, where the remains of food were piled up to attract the wild beasts to the traps.

Soon the two big-strong men came; soon they lifted Camiú by
his arms and legs, and walked along an open trail, with Ua (the
hunter) leading them. The old man swung, bent-body; his arms
and legs were held tightly, and he was hanging. The frail-old man
was being carried by big-strong men, up the long path to a
marked place which Ua pointed out: "There." Then the strong
men sat Camiú on a mound of shells, and tied him with strong
fibers from a tree. The entire body of the voiceless old man trembled; the bone of his shrunken mouth banged in his toothless chin.
the strong men turned their backs, followed Ua, and returned
along the path their feet had made until they reached the village
again.

Camiú, the old-man-alone tied up on the shell-mound, waited
for death. He sat with two huge eyes which grew outside their
accustomed holes and tried to flee, dragging behind them the poor
withered body empty of flesh and swollen with fear.

A dark shadow peeked from behind the closest green-plants; it
looked like a dark animal. Camiú gasped, chilling his entire carcass through his throat. Many shadows appeared after this one,
coming from behind and from the sides. Camiú became all ears,
in terrified attention. The sounds were mixed with others.

Camiú's head rapidly classified them: the snapping of a plant, the flight of a beast, the dragging along of another. Camiú's head was tired, and the noise grew within his ears. He sought with his eyes for the source of the noise, which hid behind things in the dark shadows. Camiú's fear climbed up his skin like a soft, clinging beast. His eyes wanted to flee the darkness, and they went farther out of their holes. Soon the darkness let him see no more.

Everything was black. Camiú, half dizzy, ached in his bones from sitting in one position. The old-old man lost a little of his awareness of things because he was tired.

Suddenly he woke up!

From the darkness he heard a slight crackling which came near, disguised and careful.

The old-man-without-voice opened his entire mouth into an enormous hole. Cold dribbling worms, which come from the fear of bodies and empty them of everything they have, descended from his shivering skin.

The steps came closer and closer; the old man sensed in the great darkness of silence the smell of the wild beast, and then its breath.

Mamazu and Tumai picked up the strange-herb with their fingers, and felt it. Tumai rubbed a mashed piece on his nose; it had a strong smell. He put a small piece into his mouth and crushed it many, many times with his teeth.

Mamazu stood watching Tumai, waiting for a response. Tumai seemed to forget Mamazu. Time passed quietly. Tumai lifted his eyes and saw Mamazu's still face, which suddenly looked like a very large shriveled yellow-fruit. The shriveled-fruit opened a gap and began to speak to Tumai, who saw the red pulp of the gap deep inside the yellow-fruit. Mamazu's voice came out of the withered-fruit from the back of the red gap. Tumai opened his eyes great-wide, pointed his finger at Mamazu's face, and laughed, and laughed, and laughed. Mamazu silently took a piece of the magic-herb; he wanted to know why!

Afterwards Mamazu, an old man of an age which the fingers of many hands could not count, who dominated magic and spoke with spirits (the good and evil-companions), took the herb-that-laughs, and with Tumai went out of the hut, laughing, and laughing, and laughing. They distributed the herb to the old men of the

Great Council. They all sat down in a circle with a full gourd in the middle, and they prepared and took the magic-drink.

The men who had been angry found that things were very funny and life was very good. The old men decreed that the herb-that-laughs was magic from the spirit-friends, to free men from their tiredness. They ordered the young men to drink, and to laugh at one another all night long.

The old men and the young ones drank and laughed willingly and happily, because the magic was good. Only after laughter and sleep had taken their turn did they remember Camiú and realize that to have the magic-herb they needed the old man.

The day was white and had scarcely begun. The eye-of-fire had not yet come to cook things with heat and colors. The men, however, took their weapons and hurried to save the old-man-without-voice, who was now not an evil-spirit, but someone sent by the Companion-Spirit with good-magic. Men who took the magic-drink liked one another, thought that things and people were funny, and slept well.

When the men arrived at the faraway shell-mound where Ua prepared the traps for the wild beasts which roam around at night, and where men threw the leftovers from the village to attract the beasts, they did not go very close. They did not have to. In the place where Ua and the two strong men had left Camiú the day before, there remained only a pile of chewed bones, tied up loosely with strong fibers from trees. Camiú had carried with him on his trip to the spirits the secret of the herb-that-laughs. As a legacy he left only the strange plant with yellow-grains and red hairs, which the people of the village would one day learn to eat.

Chapter 4

Angry-spirits drink the water of men. On how to teach swollen-spirits with strong-magic, which has desired results, and to thank them for favors received. On how men were strong with the spirits and weak with the women.

The sky had not opened up its pots for many light-times, between so, so many darks. The eye-of-fire on high cooked a blue which hurt people's eyes. Below, the greens were disappearing. Many light-times between so, so many darks continued passing. The heat robbed things of their shapes and colors. The sweet-waters lazed away day by day, lowering the springs, bringing in their arms. It was time to carry out the move to the other side of the angry-waters, and the young men and their women-companions waited only for the forces to blow the other direction, to aid the arms of men in pushing the waters. Men and women who had prepared their belongings for the crossing should already be forming a new village on the other side.

And they waited.

Up high the blue slid along without obstacle; not a white-body or friendly gray one ended the people's discouragement. White-bodies and gray ones held the sky's water in their fat bellies.

The blue, thin and washed out by the fire in the eye, did not change, not even when the men painted their faces with ashes from the hearths and walked along the sand showing ashen-faces to the blue-above. Their faces became full-bellied gray-bodies full of saved-water (they pretended). Not even when they washed their dirty faces in the waters-that-run-lying-down, letting the water drip and run, as the fat gray-bodies up above ought to do, did the blue hide itself. Not even then!

Mamazu thought that something stronger ought to be done, something which would not tolerate negative responses on the part of the spirits, and would produce the desired result. When the staked plants, which the women with big-bellies cared for (because it was certain that things were born from them), began to pull in their bodies and bend their necks, Mamazu gave the order:

"Let there be dug a hole the size of three men lying down by two of the same size."

The men began the arduous work (the fire ran over their bodies until the water stopped running from them). Flat stones and sticks with stone points fastened to them served as tools.

They dug.

Strong arms dug deeper. When the ditch was ready, and the men had broken branches and stripped trunks, they surrounded the hole with a kind of hut (made of trunks and branches), and closed the gaps with more boughs. The result was a lush green false-plant.

It was pretty when it was finally ready.

Mamazu called everyone to see the finished shelter over the hole (they came). The men surrounded Mamazu, who spoke very seriously:

"The spirits of the swollen-bodies that go through the skies have not visited the village for a long time. Men have made the swollen-spirits displeased, and they have carried their waters far away. Now men ought to teach the spirits what they ought to do to return their waters."

The men nodded yes with their heads, and began to move their arms and legs in serious preparation.

Ua went off into the middle of the most mixed greenery, with Catumai and Dao-dao (two boys) behind him. The eye burned on

high, making a dark-body follow each one. The man–two-boys
walked one behind the other, the body of Catumai following the
dark-body of Ua, the body of Dao-dao following the dark-body of
Catumai, the dark-body of Dao-dao alone finishing the long-cord
of bodies, light-dark-light-dark-light-dark, of everybody together
in the middle of the mixed greenery of the tallest plants. Man-
boy-boy entered and left the forest, seeking a place where the
beasts-that-fly rest their feathers and their eggs.

"Tweet, tweet, tweet," went Dao-dao.

"Tweet, tweet, tweet," went a beast-that-flies, far off.

"Tweet, tweet, tweet." Dao-dao.

"Tweet, tweet, tweet." The beast-that-flies, nearer.

"Tweet, tweet, tweet." Dao-dao.

There was a beast-that-flies, with grand colors on its feathers,
hopping on the ground. Ua and Catumai quickly used their net for
catching fish to cover the beast-that-flies-that-hops-on-the-
ground, and it was done!

The beast beat its feathers and colors, and let out harsh,
shrieked tweets in the threads of the net. The fingers of Catumai's
small hand circled the thin neck of the beast-that-beats-feathers
and twisted, twisted until its beak turned around to the back and
then to the front of the body again from the other side. The body
of the beast went limp and stopped resisting. Dark stickiness ran
from the open beak as Catumai held up the beast by its long legs.

The man-boy-boy proceeded in a line of light-dark through the
greenery, tweeting and gathering together beasts-that-fly.

Other men and boys in other sections of the mixed greenery
did the same thing at the same time.

Each group came back to the center of the village holding by
the legs a colored handful of beasts-that-no-longer-fly. They
threw them all on a mixed-up pile of feathers and beaks so the
women could do their work.

"This work is done to convince the stubborn spirits that they
ought to open their swellings and let loose their waters!" Mamazu
understood in his head.

The blue way up in the sky was even more washed out. Malaí
sat on her feet pulling out the feathers of the beasts. The other
women also pulled out the feathers of the beasts, and formed a
pile with them. The crude skin of the beasts appeared underneath;
a dead-mound of beasts-naked-in-their-skins grew next to the
living-mound of feathers. Malaí thought in her head that Karincai

did not like to take the beasts-that-fly from their natural place, which was on high. Were there not enough wild beasts down here below, and enough fish and shells?

"But the feathers? The men need them."

The swollen-bellies of stubborn spirits did not come. The magic-shelter was ready for calling them, and now the feathers which were needed were too; there were so many of them.

While these preparations were being carried out, Kotia and Kotiatí had visions as they slept. They dreamed about the father of their father's father, who said that a very angry spirit had drunk all the water that was meant for men. Kotia and Kotiatí had been born together at one time, and as always when this happened with men, they had the power to change the nature of the waters-that-fall-from-on-high and to calm the eye-of-fire. Because Kotia and Kotiatí had been one in two, with face and body identical, no one could know which was which if it were not that a fish one day had carried off the tip of one of Kotia's fingers. And so Kotia was the one who had almost one finger less than the whole-hand of Kotiatí. That was how they were told apart.

The two, who had been summoned by Mamazu, came into the middle of the village, as did all the men and children. The women brought nets filled to the top with feathers. Everyone came close to the hut built over the hole which they had dug the size of three men lying down by two of the same size.

Mamazu called the name of each of the tribe's old and young men; they all entered the hole, each one as he was called. Kotia and Kotiatí went down, carrying with them two large stones which they carefully put on the ground in the middle. Then they went back up to stay with Mamazu on the edge of the hole. Mamazu held in his hands an implement made of long-thin bone with a sharpened point. The two brothers hung the nets full of colored feathers over the heads of the old and young men, who were all inside the hole.

The children outside the hut pushed with their hands on one another, because they all wanted to see through the empty spaces between the boughs. Some of them glued their eyes to the spaces; others shoved the ones in front, and knocked them down. Each one put an eye to an eye-space, as soon as another left a gap. Some climbed up on the thickest trunks, so that a bunch of children hung up high.

Kotia and Kotiatí were learning the secrets of the spirits from

Mamazu because they were two-the-same with resulting powers, and even more because they envisioned things while they slept. That was why Kotia and Kotiatí extended their arms to Mamazu, who inserted the sharpened point of the long-thin-bone into the blue-lines that run down the arms of men, just as water runs down the body of the earth. The sharpened-bone pierced the fine skin of the blue-lines. Mamazu stretched the holes to enlarge them slightly, and dark red spurted out of the blue-lines of the two arms of Kotia and the two arms of Kotiatí.

Kotia and Kotiatí held their arms over the heads of the old men and the young ones, who were all standing below in the hole. Red-drops which ran from the arms of the two men were falling, flowing onto the eyes and mouths and shoulders and arms of the men below. Kotia and Kotiatí walked around the sides of the hole with their arms extended, giving forth their red-drops which flowed without stopping onto the heads and eyes and mouths and shoulders of the men.

Then they loosened the nets, and the feathers fell onto the men. They fell colorfully, covering wet and sticky bodies, heads, eyes, mouths, and arms, while Mamazu spoke: "May the spirits of the swollen-bellies learn that they ought to open their swellings and again let loose their waters over the village of men, who are showing them how to do it. Not even the most stubborn and furious spirits can fail to respond to this powerful magic!" The feathers were (pretending) the swollen-bellies, and the red-water which they took from their own bodies represented the water which everyone hoped would fall to the earth from on high.

When they finished their circuit of the sides of the hole, Kotia and Kotiatí fell down with weak bodies. Mamazu aided them, tying each arm of the two men with fibers which he tightened firmly. Kotia and Kotiatí took into their mouths, which were white-without-color, a strong drink which flushed their faces and lifted their bodies, for they had a difficult path ahead of them. But Kotia and Kotiatí were strong. They picked up the two big stones they had put down in the hole, settled them on their shoulders, and carried them outside the village.

Children jumped down from the clusters hanging from the trunks, children left the spaces where their eyes had peeked, children ran behind, jumping and looking for small stones which they put on their shoulders in imitation. They were swollen-bellies (they pretended) which were coming in response to the call of the men of the village, now that Kotia and Kotiatí had shown how to do it, carrying on their shoulders the stones–stubborn-spirits, showing how swollen-bellies up above ought to move.

The two men with the stones on their shoulders walked a very long distance without stopping. The children stopped along the way, put down their stones, and returned to the village.

The blue way up high was acquiring an increasingly heavy color, and the eye-of-fire was rolling away. Kotia and Kotiatí tripped on their own tired feet, but continued walking and walking until they arrived at their destination. They found a very tall green-plant, the tallest and fattest in the area. It was in a place which was a very long space-time from the village, in the middle of a bare spot of ground, near which a little sweet-water ran in the bottom of an almost dry pathway. The men climbed the dark trunk to the highest spot which could bear the weight of the two together, and there they put the two stones, as the swollen-bellies ought also to climb up high in the sky. The two stones were swollen-bellies (they pretended) and the stubborn spirits should already be much more gentle!

Kotia and Kotiatí climbed down the fat-trunk and turned their steps toward the village again.

The men, with the feathers of the beasts-that-fly stuck to them, walked through the village after the two-equal-brothers had gone to carry the stones–swollen-bellies far away. The men went out to search for the remains of still-waters, deep springs of water which were almost empty, where small beasts which fly and suck men's blood swarmed above. The feather-men took handfuls of earth and threw them into the middle of the eyes-of-water, taking apart the clumps with their fingers and letting the dirt fall. More than this the stubborn spirits could not stand! Next the men fell-themselves into the water, leaving in it their borrowed feathers. Afterwards they returned to the village behind Kotia and Kotiatí, who were stumbling back.

When all the men were again in the middle of the village, Mamazu gave an order: "Tear down the hut, just as we want men to tear down the ill-will of the stubborn spirits, who hold on to the waters in the gray-bodies far away in the sky."

All of the men then went off running; they banged with the tops of their heads on the branches and green boughs of the hut, so that it shook. They turned their steps back, and got ready for a new run. They all ran together, coming from all sides, and with

the tops of their heads again banged the branches and green
boughs, parts of which broke off into the hole this time.

The men turned their steps back and tried again. With their
bodies bent in half toward the front and their hands behind their
backs, they started a new run with the tops of their heads pointed
toward the middle of the hut. This time the branches fell into the
hole with a creaking sound, and only the thick trunks remained.
Then the men, already half dizzy from banging their heads against
the stubbornness of the spirits, stopped, and furiously tore down
the trunks which formed the bones of the hut.

Now they just had to wait until the sky covered itself with
swollen-bellies full of water!

Catumai and Dao-dao played in deep-eyes which had only a
small amount of water. They speared little fish with small
sharpened-sticks, or they funneled them by directing them with a
braid made of fibers, which the two held, one on each side. They
squeezed the fish to the edge of the water, some tangled up in the
brilliance of others. Catumai and Dao-dao used their hands to
catch what remained of the shivers (all little fish) which slid rapidly with the water between their fingers. Laughing, they cut off
the heads with their teeth, spit them out, and devoured the rest.

But Catumai–Dao-dao's game was made easier by the low
water. It was simpler now to wade into the half-gone springs
which had almost no water, and to hold out their hands together.
The fish, some already swimming stomach up, went in without
resisting at all. Finally, Catumai–Dao-dao's game lost its fun, on
a morning in which the shrunken-eye-empty-of-water woke only
to the dead, still brilliance of all the fish there were.

Catumai and Dao-dao returned to the village with burning
throats, for the sweet-water which constantly falls from the rocks
had dried, and they did not see a living-eye of water along the
path. All dead!

Mamazu went up on the shell-mound and stayed there without
going down again to his hut for the whole length of a dry and hot
darkness.

The men had done everything-everything as it ought to be
done. Mamazu waited. Kotia and Kotiatí went up and stayed with
Mamazu on top of the shell-mound for yet another hot and dry
darkness. It was then that the thundering began to come from the
huge throat of the darkness, as some spirit on high announced a
decision.

Mamazu, Kotia, and Kotiatí raised their eyes to the little white holes in the darkness above, and waited for the great-throat to repeat the thundering. They waited a short time. The familiar noise repeated, now coming from somewhere closer, although they could not see where it originated.

Later round-bodies came to fill up the little holes in the darkness way up high. In a short time the swollen-bodies took up all the space which the light showed. Only then did Mamazu and the two-equal-brothers come down from the shell-mound.

They all waited.

Malaí went out of the hut and lifted her face to get it wet; big drops of sweet-water were falling, big and well separated. Afterwards the quantity grew and the size diminished, until they turned into fine threads which danced on one side and the other, all together in the hands of the spirit-force that carried the leaves to the ground and pulled the sands along.

Malaí ran shouting, "Did you see, Karincai? . . . Did you see how the stubborn spirits had to give back the waters to the people?"

Karincai saw. But Karincai thought in his head that the water had to fall at any rate, whether the men had or had not done what they did. Karincai scratched his chest with his fingernails, taking off the dust and salt which were always glued to him, while the sweet-waters poured down. Karincai, pleased, spread the good-water with his fingers over his chest, his arms, his face, his legs.

Malaí was shining all over, with the water running down the shape of her body and her hair stuck to her. Karincai thought it was good to look at Malaí, thought that looking at Malaí awoke inside him heat which gave him a great, great deal of strength. Karincai felt that he was strong, very-very strong, with a desire to crush things, to squeeze things. Malaí leaned against his chest, saying, "See, Karincai?"

Karincai saw that the strength would no longer fit inside him. He lifted Malaí, hung her over his shoulder, and ran to the beach, the strength exploding inside him. The water ran down Malaí's hair and continued its thread on Karincai's body. Malaí moved her hand, caressing; it made him tremble, but not from weakness. Karincai felt great strength.

Karincai arrived at the immense wet beach, where the angry-water made a huge noise when it went back down. Karincai lost his desire to run, threw Malaí down there on the ground in the sand, and threw himself down as well.

And the water kept falling down on top of them.

Mamazu went out of his hut and lifted his face to get it wet. The fine threads fell, dancing from side to side. Mamazu let his old body, dry like the plants, receive the sweet-water. It was good. It was good to see all the men and women and children leaving their huts and putting out their faces to get wet!

Kotia and Kotiatí also walked in the sweet-water. It was good. The plants would become green again and open their colored-eyes, and the dead-eyes of water would be filled with brilliant fish. The sweet-water would fall from the stones as before. The force in the air would blow from the right direction, so that the men and their women-companions could go ahead, with everything that was theirs, to form a new village a space-time away on the angry-water, as the spirits had determined.

Now that the spirits had listened to the pleas of the people, they had to be thanked. Therefore Mamazu ordered thanks which were certain to please the spirits.

With the water still streaming over them, Mamazu made a circle with Kotia and Kotiatí. He held the long-thin-bone in his hands. The men and children formed a long-cord of men and children waiting one behind the other.

The first man came close to Mamazu, who had Kotia and Kotiatí on either side. The first man opened his arms and bared his hairy chest, which was wet from the sweet-water running down him. Mamazu came near with his sharpened long-bone and scratched the skin on the chest of the first man. The red which comes from inside and the sweet-water spurted out together. Mamazu opened more red-eyes all around on his skin. The red-water ran down the body of the first man. Then he showed to the sky his chest with torn skin (the water falling) so the swollen-spirits could see how brave men are!

The second man bared his hairy chest for Mamazu to scratch. He did it, and the sweet-water ran red down the chest of the second man when he ran off, showing it to the sky. The third man was a boy; he revealed his small chest, then pushed ahead, clenched his teeth, and did not move. Mamazu inserted the cutting-bone into his skin, and tore it sideways. The red burst forth alive, flowing with the sweet-water on the smooth chest of the third man-boy who was brave. Next the fourth man took his place in front of Mamazu. After the skin had been opened on the chests of all the men (the children pushed for their turns, each one wanted his; it was as though they were going to get a good-mouthful to chew), they ran around washing themselves in the sweet-water which fell from above, until the red stopped coming from inside their chests.

Thus a response was made to the stubborn spirits of the swollen-bellies, who were now satisfied with men.

The next day they all moaned, for the new skin hurt and pulled. They forgot to be brave at the hands of their women-companions, as they had been brave of face and chest before the spirits. And they complained (ow, ows ran through the entire village), the men and boys. Tumai told them to put on themselves plants, which, if well cooked, could make the tightening skin sleep for a time.

Hurting men were always angry; the women-companions tolerated it, except Ima, who had fled from Ua and hid herself well. Ua became irate and threw all of Ima's things out of the hut: cups and gourds; strings with ornaments of bone and shell; long-thin bones with a hole in the end of each one, used to sew skins. Ua angrily threw it all outside and kicked at it with his foot. Afterwards he went into the hut alone and moaned loudly, for the tightening skin on his chest was on fire, and hurt.

After a time counted by the fingers of a whole-hand, the tightening skin of the men's chests still hurt. Later they became less angry, and brave again, when the new skin closed in reddish lines.

One day Ua went out to hunt the big wild beasts, which he did not fear, and met Ima, who waited along the path. Ua thought that he would be angry, but Ima had such a way about her of someone who had done nothing that Ua thought, "If I get angry now, afterwards there is the work of undoing the anger." Ima made an open face to Ua's closed face. Ua also opened his face to Ima, and went on ahead; Ima walked behind him. When Ua dug in the ground to make a trap, Ima brought leaves which were cool and damp from the night, and gave them to Ua to cover the prepared trap. Ua thought that it was good to feel again the cool-damp leaves in Ima's arms, and he continued his work.

Catumai and Dao-dao were now brilliant fish who swam through the eye-of-sweet-water, from one side to the other.

Malaí ran her soft fingers along the tightened skin of the red lines on Karincai's chest.

And the greens were again green.

Chapter 5

The trip to the other side: those who stay and those who go. The beginning of the new village. Plants-that-harm and plants-that-cure. Dark-feet and evil-eyes spy from behind plants. On how men learn things.

The people prepared themselves for the important trip.

Since those who start a new village ought to be young men, Mamazu decided that the old men would stay, and that he would stay with them, Kotia and Kotiatí would go, carrying with them their powers, along with Ua's spears and the nets and tools of the fishermen, Karincai and Kaúma among them.

Young women carried things to the trunks-that-float. Malaí had her arms full of bowls and cups, one on top of the other; the hot-soft sand was difficult beneath her feet, and she could not see the path. Catumai and Dao-dao saw Malaí coming, with a body which was only cups and gourds and had no head. Malaí did not see Catumai and Dao-dao, who hid behind the trunk-that-floats.

Malaí went along with difficulty, because the soft-hot of the ground hurt her feet and the cups and gourds covered the pathway of her eyes. She hurried toward the trunk-that-floats, which she knew was pulled up waiting.

When Malaí lowered her body and let go of bowls and cups, Catumai–Dao-dao quickly pulled the trunk-that-floats into the water. Bowls and cups, bowls and cups, bowls and cups rolled and spread out over the ground, which the water was already getting wet. The water licked everything, and the bowls and cups floated off. Malaí screamed with her mouth and with her arms, and jumped with her legs. Catumai–Dao-dao opened their faces and stuck out their red tongues and laughed. Ima, who was coming in a pile of hammocks, dropped everything and ran off behind them. Malaí ran after them as well, but Catumai–Dao-dao moved their legs with such speed that no one caught them. Suddenly Catumai hit his foot on a stone and fell flat on his face.

Then they grabbed him.

Malaí grabbed Catumai's hair (Dao-dao watching from far off) while Ima grabbed the legs of the struggling boy. Malaí, with Catumai's hair held in her fingers, came close to his face. She opened her mouth and bit Catumai's ear hard. He gave a roar from his throat and scratched Malaí's arms with his fingernails. Malaí held Catumai's arms beneath her folded legs, pulled his hair hard, and bit his nose and his other ear. Catumai managed to give Ima a hard kick, and Dao-dao came from behind and pulled Malaí by the neck so she fell. Catumai freed, ran off, and Dao-dao did too.

Catumai's nose and ears had the marks of Malaí's teeth. The red ran from them, and they were very hot.

Malaí and Ima went into the angry-water to grab the trunk-that-floats, which rose and fell softly, but the cups and bowls were already far-off dots, for the water had carried them hopelessly away.

Other women came with more cups and bowls, long bamboo sticks and many other things belonging to the men, hammocks, the skins of beasts, and the everything-of-everyone, and put it all into the trunks-that-float.

The loaded trunks went off with the men inside. The women and children waited, sitting on the damp edge of the water, which came up to their feet and even their bodies. Little boys dove in while they waited. Old men and women brought some white-roots in big nets, and some dead-beasts hanging by the feet on long poles.

Mamazu watched with eyes full of a brilliance which the light of day had not put in them. He saw women laughing and letting down their hair, and children jumping in the angry-water on just one foot. He saw, so far away that they were just dots, the trunks which carried away the men on the first trip, taking their belongings. Mamazu thought that his time was already very long, and that he was as tired inside as he was in his legs. He sat down on the edge of a rock, and wanted to sleep a very just sleep, with the spirits resting over his head.

By the time the trunks returned empty, with the men pushing aside the waters, the yellow-eye had made a hole right in the middle of the blue up above and spread out light with great yellow strands toward every side.

The women prepared the fish which the boys had brought up from their dives, and when the men got out of the trunks, they all ate.

Leaving behind the old men and women, the young ones went off together. There were not many, only a few fingers-of-a-hand of men and young women, and their children. (Some others had stayed at the old village, to defend the old men and women, and to continue life.) They were not many, but the best, for they had much ahead of them. They got out of the trunks-that-float, which they left overturned so the backs would dry, and walked along an enormous section of sand which was so big it would not fit into a single glance.

Around the enormous curved-white-bones of what had been the blue-animal, the men collected dark pieces of hanging meat, which the white-salt had dried over time. There was a great deal of meat. They had had such good luck that no wild animals had crossed the very long, white section of sand to get there, and the beasts-that-fly, because of the great heat, had not gone there either. This would be the place for the new shell-mound. The new village, however, would be some distance away. They walked and walked along the loose sand up to the edge of the plants which begin low with only green-hair, and grow in size, spreading out among many big-trunks with their branches all around. There at the entrance to the greenery, on the edge of a little burbling sweet-water, the men wet the feet of the new village.

Kaúma and Ua went out with their stone cutting-tools and another companion, Tagima, who had been a young man for a short time. Tagima had thin hairs on his body, which had barely finished growing, and had long arms and legs. They entered the forest on a trail where the big-trunks they had gone to cut were scattered. Catumai, Dao-dao, and some smaller boys collected branches, which would be used to build the first-big-hut of everybody-together as protection from the wild animals. It had to be finished before things were turned off in men's eyes.

Kaúma banged a very heavy pointed-stone, holding it with two hands together; he hit hard and made a white smile of an opening in the bark of a big-trunk. It was a half-tall plant (one man standing on another of the same size) and had fingers and fingernails beneath the trunk, which opened to the earth on all sides. Men could sit on the nailed-fingers which dug into the ground, securing the big-trunk. But the nailed-fingers could not hold up the trunk when Kaúma banged hard, and banged and banged. When he was tired he handed the tool to Ua, who finished splitting the mouth of the opening until he had separated the trunk in two. It fell hard to the side, full of branches and noises.

Catumai and Dao-dao seized the branches, and the smaller boys cut them off with cutting-stones (white-milk ran out). They piled them together and carried them on their backs to the good place to begin the new village.

Catumai put piles of branches up on his shoulders, Dao-dao did the same, and the smaller boys ran behind imitating them. Ua, Kaúma, and Tagima carried the trunks. They planted the hut in a good place. Everybody helped, braiding branches. When the hut was almost ready (the eye in the sky had moved to the side), one little boy stood in a corner and began to yell.

Dao-dao shook the smaller boy: "Stop that shouting!" The little boy showed his mouth: "Ow, ow!" Dao-dao saw chunks of separated and cut skin in the mouth of the smaller boy, and ran to call people.

The men finished the first-hut. The young women prepared a big hearth with stones. Between the stones they set up the dead-beasts which hung by all-their-feet on a long pole. In the middle of the dry wood and the reds of the fire they threw some white-roots. The dry wood of the big tree did not catch fire easily; it gave off dark smoke which spread out and burned their eyes.

The smaller boy lying on the ground on leaves was becoming red-hot in his head and weak in his body. His cut mouth with chunks of loose skin hanging down hurt the smaller boy, who was very hot. He saw horrible hallucinations, and his body shook.

Malaí had put some white-roots into a small eye-of-water.
The white-roots ought to stay and stay there, until later when
the women could squeeze them and make cakes to eat. White-
roots like these grew plants with branches and leaves the half-
height of a big man, sometimes more. After one or two
hands-full-of-fingers of white-eyes of time, many other white-
roots would hang on the branches. The women would take
them all off and bury some, so everything could begin again.
The white-roots could not be eaten, nor their water drunk,
without first cooking them on the fire. It was strange; this was
true only for people, because the wild animals could eat and
drink as much as they wanted of the white-roots, without being
harmed. But people were hurt by the uncooked white-roots.
Once cooked, the white-roots lost their evil-spirit, and when the
women ground them in their bowls or squeezed them, they
became very good. They were not difficult for the men and
women to store; they kept well in sweet-water or in earth.

Malaí went to get a white-root already soft-dark in the water
(Kotia and Kotiatí ordered it), because the heat of the little boy
did not cool off for a long time.

Kotia took a dark-wet white-root which already smelled
strongly, and threw it into the fire. The dark wood showed no
more red tongues; it threw off a dark red only when Kotia blew on
it. The white-root was becoming darker and darker. Kotia turned
and turned it with a long-bone until the whole white-root he had
put in the fire turned into black-root. When this happened, Kotia
chipped and chipped at it to make sand of black-root, which he
mixed with water. He gave it to the little boy to drink, to take
away the hotness.

Malaí and Tira, a girl-woman, were on the sand which had no
end, only hills on the edges made of the sand itself. Tira took
some shells, wet them, and used a small stick to take the soft
beasts from inside them. Then she washed them in the angry-
water.

Malaí opened them, and Tira threaded the shells on a fiber
with a fine-bone, which she poked through holes in the shells.
When they were finished, the ornaments sang together in a tin-
kling dance. They were lovely!

Tira covered herself with the strings-of-shells (round, prickly,

and long ones, white, pink, and mottled ones). Tira danced the
shells and made them sing on the new curves of her body.

Malaí laughed, clapping her hands together. The pretty shell-
ornaments made music with one another on Tira's neck when she
danced, and Malaí laughed.

Behind a big-plant, which followed others in a line on top of
the sand hill, the dark-feet of a hidden body watched in careful
silence.

Dark-feet without noise, only prints, were digging their shape
into the sand, watching Tira, Tira dancing and the shells singing
on one another. The dark-feet, which carried two eyes which were
shining malevolently, went away leaving prints without noise all
around in the sand.

The dark-feet went lightly-cautiously around the new village,
where the men worked on new huts.

Kaúma and Tagima cut some big-plants which would serve as
the bones for the new huts. Kaúma showed Tagima that the big-
plants which he cut had the age of their time counted inside their
trunks. Inside the thick bark were many, many circles one inside
the other, inside another, inside another, each one showing a
complete-time lived by the green-plant. By counting them you
could know the age of the plant. Tagima listened and learned.

The green-plant had leaves which were not very rounded and
had teeth on the edges and crosshatched lines inside. They were
thick, with short hairs which were rough on the points of Tagima's fingers. They were held on by small stems.

When Tagima cut a stem, white-milk ran out and stuck to his
fingers. Tagima tasted it; Kaúma yelled, "No!"

Tagima dropped the leaf and focused his attention on the
green, yellowish green, and purple swollen-fruits which appeared
among the leaves. He stretched out his hand and picked one; it
was smooth, with a thin shell. He tightened his fingers and the
soft-fruit broke in two. Inside there were fine, delicate threads of
pink-color, which looked like a small flower turned inside out.
Tagima submerged his mouth in it, and it was very sweet. He and
Kaúma chose many purplish fruits, which were the good ones.

The darkness descended from the shadows and crept along the
ground. Kaúma suddenly thought he heard leaves being stepped
on. He stopped to listen, the air held inside his chest so he could
hear better. The noise of footsteps glided softly, cautiously; they
were made by a large beast or a human-person. Kaúma went on,

holding his sharpened-stone for knocking down trunks, with Tagima behind him. Walking through the greenery, he sought something, seeking and seeking, with Tagima behind him.

Kaúma walked around the green hills of plants, with Tagima
behind him. Tagima saw it!

Tagima grabbed Kaúma: "Look." He pointed.

Kaúma looked.

Kaúma saw that the ground behind a big green-plant was trodden in the shape of feet; the footprints were made by human-
people, not by any beast.

It was very quiet all around; the end of day awoke no sound.

Kaúma and Tagima walked through the green-forest, seeking
and seeking, but did not see any human-people. They went on to
the village carrying their cut trunks and collected fruit.

The dark-feet planted themselves high up on a branch of a
big-trunk. Two eyes, which sparkled malevolently and saw everything, hung suspended.

The root-drink which Kotia had prepared made the little boy's
hotness go down, but his cut mouth with chunks of flesh falling
off did not get better. Now thick-white-water ran from the chunks
of flesh, it hurt more, and little buzzing beasts flew around both-
ering the boy.

When Tagima showed that his mouth was also cut, with
chunks of skin forming bumps, Kaúma remembered: "Tagima
cutting the stem of the leaf of the big-plant, white-milk flowing
out, sticking to his fingers, Tagima tasting it, and Kaúma saying,
'No!'"

The day before, the small boy, with Catumai–Dao-dao, had
also attacked the leafy boughs with cutting-stones. The white-
milk had run out of them. The boys had piled up branches and
carried them on their backs to the good place to begin a new
village. Kaúma remembered well, and now he pointed out to
Kotia that the chunks of flesh separating in Tagima's mouth were
like the chunks of flesh in the small boy (which were now much
worse).

The old shell-mound of Mamazu did not have this plant. However, Kotia thought there ought to be another thing to take away
the dangerous effect of the poisonous white-milk. Mamazu had
taught that each evil-spirit had an opposing good-spirit.

Kotia greatly missed having the wisdom of the old-old man

with him; for the first time he saw the great emptiness that was new-space!

The men put the women and children into the now-ready hut of everybody-together. The spirits up above were already throwing down the dark cover which hid everything from view.

Kotia brought together Kotiatí (who was his equal-brother), Kaúma (who figured out clever things), Karincai (who took his own ideas from his head), and Ua (who was strong, to defend the village), and formed with them the Great Council.

In the place-spot which would be the new shell-mound, Kotia–Kotiatí and the other men sat together around a lit fire, to resolve the first difficult problem of the new village.

Many other plants, Kotiatí remembered, have white-milk which we know is poisonous. Tumai, an old man who understood a great deal about the plants in the other village, had said, "Poisonous plant kills; poisonous plant cures with its own venom." Kotiatí remembered a long-thin plant which had only a few branches at the top, and leaves similar to those of the poisonous plant. It also had fruit which grew in bunches; men and beasts-that-fly would eat the fruit when the sweetness spurted out of it. Kotiatí remembered that Tumai stepped on the seeds and pieces of rind from this plant, trampled and trampled it until the juice was released from inside it. He put it on top of the sick parts of men. It had helped even old openings in the flesh to dry quickly.

Without losing more time, Kaúma returned his steps to the place of the big-plants, to fetch seeds and pieces of shell to help Tagima and the small boy.

Kaúma searched between trunks and trunks of many plants for that one plant which would help to heal wounds. That plant ought to exist; it ought to be someplace. It seemed (he thought in his head) that he had seen that plant in some place! Kaúma searched and searched, going through the most dense greenery.

Suddenly Kaúma saw and recognized a tall-plant like that of the old village, and made his legs move more quickly. Kaúma came close to the plant and hit its trunk hard with a pointed-stone which the women had sharpened *(bang!)*.

Kaúma jumped backwards in surprise at what he saw: The trunk was empty inside, just a shell. Suddenly, a multitude of little-dark-beasts which stung ferociously came out of it with the noise of a hissing fire. They came out and came out from inside the empty shell of the trunk, and did not stop coming. It looked like a dark moving wave. When Kaúma suddenly awoke from his shock, he already had beasts climbing up his feet and his legs, and stinging him with burning pain.

Kaúma ran like a crazy person, with the dark-beasts clinging to his skin and climbing up his legs. It was a black wave, pinching and hissing. Kaúma swatted with his hands to try to knock the beasts from his legs, but the beasts stung Kaúma's hands. Kaúma fell and rolled along the ground to the ribbon-of-water which wet the feet of the plants. Kaúma rolled inside the ribbon-of-water, letting loose from his throat a rough sound (more like that of a beast) of shock and fear.

Kaúma returned to the village with his feet and legs swollen and red. Now he too needed medicine. He told the men that the plant-that-cures existed, but that furious small-beasts, which hiss when they move and move at a speed which eyes cannot follow, guarded the trunk of the plant. He said that the trunk was empty inside, except for those beasts!

Several men carrying lit torches then went into the forest, in a line one behind the other. They found the place, as Kaúma had said, but the trunk was quiet when they arrived, without a shadow of little-dark-beasts. The smile that Kaúma's rock had made in the trunk still showed its open throat. Inside it was empty, just a shell, as Kaúma had said.

The first man came with his torch and put the fire into the open gash in the empty trunk. He threw the torch all the way inside.

In no time the crackling of fire split the trunk down the middle. From inside it a dark and boiling wave of terrible-little-dark-beasts exploded to all sides, and spread out like black fire all around on the ground. The second man, already awakened from his surprise, used his torch to cut off the path where the black-wave advanced. They threw dry branches on top ("Quickly!"), and the third man threw his torch too, making a belt of fire around them. The little-black-beasts twisted, their stingers out. As soon as the fire died and everything was very quiet, the first man took pieces of husk from the empty trunk. He and the others took it back to the village.

*   *   *

Kotia prepared the plant-that-cures.

He mashed the bark with a stone. The bark from the trunk gave off juice from inside, forming a paste. Kotia then did as Tumai had done, for now Kotia was the Tumai of the new shell-mound, as Kotiatí was the Mamazu of the new village.

Kotia carried the paste-that-cures to spread on the wounds of the sick men.

Inside the large hut, Kaúma's big red legs and feet and hands, now full of bumps, were stretched out.

Kotia talked to his own ear, saying that now everything was going wrong. The angry-spirits seemed to be annoyed with the village, since Tagima and the small boy were sick in their mouths, and Kaúma had those feet and hands and legs.

Kotia talked to his own ear while he spread the paste-that-cures in the mouths of Tagima and the small boy, and on the legs and hands and feet of Kaúma, who was now cold, and whose entire body shivered. Kaúma's legs had red places which hurt for one dark-time and yet another. Afterwards they returned to being Kaúma's legs and feet and hands, as they had been before. The mouths of Tagima and the small boy dropped off white skin, as a beast sheds its shell, and showed new skin underneath.

The men then knew that white-milk from the big-plant makes sores in the mouth, and that the trunks of the plant-that-cures are full of dark-beasts which sting the skin and can leave a man with an enormous, reddened body.

This way men learned things, in their mouths, on their legs, in their flesh, and on their skin. Thus they learned and recounted for their sons and the sons of their sons.

This way they did not err again.

Chapter 6

*No one may come close to Tira, girl-woman who is going
to become a young woman. Of how the dark-smooth-man
took Malaí to the strange-village. Faces painted with
black designs.*

Tira, a girl-woman, had to stay in a small hut which her father
had built in a clearing among the green-plants, somewhat far from
the village. Tira was afraid, because some horrible thing was happening to her. The women of the village had all hovered around
her, talking a great deal and shaking their heads. Tira's mother-
woman had come and said that she should get ready to go away.

Tira knew that girls went away in the other village, and remained locked up while they became young women. Tira did not
know the way of the have-to-go-away. Could not anyone become
a young woman right in the village?

Tira wanted to ask, but she was afraid. No one asked if Tira
was afraid. The girl-woman's father put down his pole for catching fish and went into the middle of the green thick-trunks to
build a hut.

Afterwards all the women went away and left Tira alone, and

the men looked as if they were also afraid. Yes, it was with fear that they looked at Tira. She felt the men's fear, and it turned her own fear into terror.

Tira waited alone at the entrance to the green-plants, waiting for her father as her mother had told her. Her mother-woman would not allow Tira to enter their own hut in the village.

Salt fell from the eyes of the girl-woman; it was streaming down her face. "Why doesn't Mother-woman let Tira go into the hut anymore?"

Tira lowered her head, and her little hand grasped the pretty shell necklaces which she and Malaí had made. Who knows, maybe if she gave this pretty necklace to Mother-woman, she would let Tira go into the hut. The big-darkness had already arrived, and Tira's father had still not returned to the village.

Tira called her mother-woman. Freeing a pretty shell necklace from her breast, she extended it toward her mother's neck. The face of Tira's mother-woman became very sad; she said no and went away. Tira cried aloud, with her necklace in her hands, and the woman went to cry quietly inside the hut.

Malaí, who saw everything, slowly came near. Malaí knew that Tira had to stay alone until she had become a young woman, and understood that no one could touch her or come near.

Tira cried hoarsely and called to Malaí. She held out her necklace, but no one could touch the things belonging to Tira, a girl-woman who would soon be a young woman. The things of a girl-woman who would soon be a young woman could be harmful, could kill beasts, shrivel plants, or leave people sick! Malaí knew that. Malaí spoke gently. She explained that Tira should be patient while she turned into a young woman, and said that she understood.

Tira's father arrived and called the girl-woman, telling her to stay behind him. Mother-woman brought a stone bowl with a fire lit inside it (the tongue-of-fire danced in the fat of the great-blue-animal), and brought a dried fish and a gourd of sweet-water. She put everything on the ground near Tira.

The girl-woman picked up the fish and the water; Tira's father picked up the light and went on ahead.

Malaí saw the long-thin legs of the girl-woman disappear in the darkness behind the thick-hairy legs of her father-man as they took the path outside the village.

Malaí felt a tightness in her throat. She knew that the girl-woman would be very frightened locked up alone for many days in the hut in the middle of the thick green-plants. She ran to ask Kotia to let her be the one to bring water and fish while Tira was imprisoned and no one could touch her or even look in her eyes.

Tira's father left the girl-woman inside a small hut closed on the outside, with no space for looking out bigger than the small gaps in the branches. The girl-woman glued her eyes to the holes and saw her father, who was always very good and spoke gently with her, go away without saying anything or even looking back. He was afraid that his eyes would meet a glance from Tira's eyes through the gaps between the branches.

Tira sat on the ground, ate the fish and drank the water, and lay down on a pile of dry leaves, closing her eyes and ears tightly. She remembered the things that Malaí had explained: that the time for her to be imprisoned there would pass quickly, that her father-man would come soon to take Tira back to the village, and that the young-woman Tira would return to the village more beautiful than Tira the girl-woman had been.

A very long time seemed to pass for Tira inside the hut. The fish and water were gone. Her fear had already been the same for so long that she could no longer be afraid, only tired. The hut was small; Tira had already tried to put her body in all the positions she could, and now she could scarcely move. Her back and her legs ached, and Malaí had not come as she had promised. If Malaí came, they could talk. Malaí could not come near her, nor could she touch Malaí, but she just wanted to talk and Malaí to answer. Tira spoke aloud to herself then, just to hear a voice, and she thought it was nice to speak out loud to herself. She told stories which she had heard in the village, and when she ran out of stories she spoke out loud the names of the people in the village. She spoke of the beasts, the plants, and the things she knew, until there was nothing more to speak of. Then Tira held her aching stomach and cried silently.

Malaí had gone to take dried fish and sweet-water to the girl-woman in the far-off hut; she could not take the meat of any beast, because it was forbidden. Malaí thought that Tira must be very tired, imprisoned in the hut, but that she would be happy soon because Tira's father would go to bring the new-young-woman back into the village.

Malaí went down the path which wandered through the thick-plants, and entered the clearing where Tira's father had built the hut. Malaí traveled on the path without hearing any noise; the dark-feet did not make any, because they were being very careful. Evil-eyes shone when Malaí passed the thick-plants which edged the clearing, and two dark-hands reached out to grab the shout which the young woman wanted to make when she saw the strange-face right in the middle of the path!

Tira was so weak that she could not stand up. She no longer finished her thoughts, and sometimes forgot what she was doing inside that hut. The pain in her stomach no longer hurt, but she thought it was quite terrible to become a young woman!

When it became completely dark in the village and Malaí did not return, Karincai, upset, called to Tira's mother-woman and asked about her.

"She went to take fish and sweet-water, that's all I know," answered the mother-woman.

The other women surrounded Karincai and the mother-woman. (Karincai kept asking.) Malaí had left a long time before, when the eye-of-fire was up above in the face of the open blue, they said!

No one knew anything. Karincai went to find Kaúma, and together the two went out to search.

Noises began to be heard in the green-plants as the two men started searching and searching, following the path which Malaí had taken. The tongue-of-fire danced in the bowl and cast all around a light full of shadows. Karincai and Kaúma studied the ground. "Where is Malaí?" When Kaúma and Karincai went down the path which wound through the thick-plants and entered the clearing (there where Tira's father had built the hut), the tongue-of-fire danced a dance mixed with the dust and leaves on the ground, with pieces of fallen fish and the gourd rolled to the side, and with the marks of many-feet prints on top of one another.

The young men stopped. The marks of the feet looked like marks Kaúma had seen when he had cut the thick-plants to build a hut. Kaúma spoke. He said that the new village was watched by eyes which no one saw, and walked around by feet which no one knew. But he, Kaúma, knew, and Tagima did too, that they had seen the marks of feet and heard the noise of footsteps the other day.

Karincai and Kaúma called to the girl-woman from a distance. Tira answered that she had not seen Malaí, that Malaí had not come, and that she, Tira, had a stomachache and a dizzy head. "When will Tira return to the hut in the village?"

The two young men searched all around, but the darkness was very deep and there was no chance of finding Malaí that way. They promised to bring fish and sweet-water to the girl-woman. She should wait, and they would come back soon with others.

Karincai and Kaúma returned their steps to the village, to fetch more men and more lights.

". . . Then the tongue-of-fire danced a dance mixed with dust and leaves on the ground, with pieces of fallen fish and the gourd rolled to the side, with the marks of many-feet prints on top of one other."

Each man in the village made a big-ear larger than the next. When Kaúma called upon Tagima to say yes, he had seen footsteps and heard noises on the previous day, they all nodded their heads and thought in them the same idea.

The men had always heard stories about men from distant villages who stole all the women from other villages and carried them away. That, however, had happened when there was fighting.

The mothers of the mothers of many of them, remembered Karincai, had come from distant villages, they too carried off by the fathers who had been the victors in many fights.

"But that was when there was fighting," Karincai recalled.

There were men who attacked villages and provoked fights just to carry off women, when their tribe was in danger of dying out, remembered Ua.

All the men looked at the other men at the same time, all thinking the same thoughts.

"Could it be that the man from a distant village who carried off Malaí was with a tribe in danger of dying out?"

Karincai felt the taste of ashes in his mouth. The darkness was already deep, and the men still did not know what to do. They waited until light could uncover the shape of things, so that they could go out very early in search of Malaí.

Kotia thought about what Mamazu would do at that hour, if it were he who had to act. Mamazu had never had things like this happening in the other village. Kotia had never heard more than stories about very long-ago events. There had never even been a fight in the village, except against big-beasts.

The men felt that something different was happening, and, upset, they thought and thought about what they ought to do.

When the light finally uncovered the shapes of things and they could clearly see the path taken by Malaí, the men cautiously went on through the middle of the greenery.

The men passed along the entire trail which they already knew, and entered new pathways which they did not know. The greens of the tall-plants acquired all the possible and impossible colors of green: yellow greens, red greens, blue greens, white greens, purple greens, orangish greens, and even green greens! But the men pushed through the path with eyes only in their ears and their senses on the dangers, and they did not see the pretty things which a laughing spirit had put on their path for them to see.

The men entered deeper and deeper into an unknown forest, following the marks of dragging feet and broken branches, signs that human-people had passed there.

The men were afraid. When the forest crackled it woke up their fears, and they thought about the dangers which they well knew could come from any side at any moment.

Malaí felt like a bundle of branches hanging over the shoulder of the strange-man, who moved his feet rapidly, like a beast. She had wanted to yell, and the strange-man had filled Malaí's mouth with leaves. This was after she had closed her teeth hard on the hand that held her face. The man pulled back his hand, moaning loudly, "Ow," and then Malaí had yelled. But the man with the very angry strange-face, clenching his teeth in anger, grabbed a handful of leaves and stuffed them into Malaí's mouth until it was full and he could hold the face of the young woman without danger of being bitten.

Then Malaí saw, with wide-open eyes, the face and body of the strange-man, all painted with black streaks. He did not have hairs on his body, as the other men did, but was smooth, and his skin glistened as though he had spread animal-fat all over his body. Malaí thought the strange-man was very ugly, and she was very frightened. But the ugly-man did not give Malaí time to be

afraid. He dragged the young woman farther and farther away,
with one hand securing her face and one arm around her waist.

Malaí's arms and legs dragged and were scraped on the trodden leaves and the dust of the trail. The strange-man, feeling her
body get heavier, let go his hold of Malaí's face and threw the
young woman on his shoulder as if she were dead prey.

Malaí spit out the leaves and yelled, yelled as much as she
wanted. Malaí's screams hit against the tall green-plants, lost
power, and died on the trail. No one in the village would hear
them. The strange-man entered new places which she did not
know. The plants were acquiring all the possible and impossible
colors of green: yellow greens, red greens, blue greens, white
greens, purple greens, orangish greens, and even green greens!
But Malaí did not see all the colors of green which a laughing
spirit had spread along the path for the happiness of people, because her eyes were imprisoned by fear and her thoughts imagined Karincai in the village when she did not return.

The strange-man-without-hair made a sharp yell, like that of a
beast-with-feathers, and a beast-with-feathers responded from
afar with a similar sharp yell.

The man took Malaí through the middle of green leaves which
did not seem to have a middle, and closed up the opening as soon
as they passed through, as though they had not been there. Other
strange-men came out from behind the trees; their bodies were
smooth and their skin glistened as though they had spread animal-
fat all over their bodies. Their faces were painted with black
streaks, and looked at Malaí with eyes which wounded her, so
that she huddled up on the shoulder of the first strange-man, like a
speared beast.

The smooth-men spoke sounds which Malaí did not understand. One pulled the girl by a leg, but the first man did not let
go. The two spoke loudly and angrily, and a third smooth-man
pointed farther off, to where there were sounds which must be
coming from their village.

And they all went there.

The smooth-man took Malaí from his shoulder and threw her
to the ground in the middle of the village. Men and women with
smooth, hairless bodies came running from all sides. They were
all painted with black marks, the men with straight lines one beside the other, the women with delicate designs. They surrounded

Malaí, who was seated on the ground, and looked at her and spoke strange sounds, all at the same time.

One woman who was more curious came close and put her fingertips on Malaí. She laughed, and moved her fingers over Malaí's body, as though she wanted to see if the new-woman were real. She laughed louder, nervously, and began to pinch Malaí hard until she screamed in pain. The smooth-man shoved the woman away with his foot and freed Malaí, who rubbed the red-marks made on her by the pinches of the woman's hand.

The smooth-man showed by his demeanor before the others that he was now Malaí's owner. He ostentatiously tied the hands and feet of the young woman, and fastened her to a tall-trunk. He waved his arms and spoke some angry words, saying that no one should come near his woman. He went away, leaving Malaí alone.

Malaí began to look at the village, which had round huts made of trunks covered with plant-fibers which were well tied down and fastened to one another. Women with children hanging on their arms and shoulders looked out suspiciously from the openings. To Malaí they all looked the same, with their identical dark faces. She could discern only one difference: There were young women and old women. The old women were all the same, with their dull hair, sagging skin, and puckered mouths. The young women were all the same, with shining hair, rounded flesh where two hanging big-fruits swung, and smooth bodies without hair. Their skin did not have the gentle redness of Malaí's but was darker, not like the calm sky before the night, but like the gray sky before water falls.

Malaí's feet and hands hurt, and she was tired of being in the same position. One of the old women looked at her with eyes different from the eyes of the others. She had the gentle manner of a beast sneaking away in the midst of the other women, and did not say anything.

The old woman passed in front of Malaí several times, like someone who did not want anything. She looked at her with shining eyes buried in a wrinkled face. Her eyes were like two luminous beasts imprisoned inside her face, and seemed not to have anything to do with the rest of her face.

When the other women had sated their curiosity and each one went to take care of her own life, the old woman made a signal to Malaí and went into a hut. Afterwards she brought out in her hands a bowl with something soft and steaming inside it, and held it out for Malaí to eat. Since the young woman was suspicious, the shrunken mouth opened in a friendly laugh, and Malaí, who was dying from weakness, dipped her fingers into the bowl. Picking up a handful of the soft, sticky paste, she brought it to her mouth, trembling with anxiety. The dough tasted good to Malaí, and she dipped in her fingers many more times, and put them in her mouth quickly, afraid that someone would come to take away the bowl which the old woman had given her. She hurried so much that the bowl fell before the paste was finished. To Malaí's great amazement, it broke into pieces, scattering reddish brown shards. Malaí picked up the thin, light pieces, turned them over and over, and tried to fit them together. The strange bowl was not made from the trunk of a plant. What was it, then? It looked like mud, but mud is soft and the bowl was hard and firm and shiny. Malaí wished that Karincai could see it. Only then did Malaí notice that all the bowls and pots which the women of the village carried back and forth full of sweet-water and soft-sticky paste were made of the same reddish brown material.

Malaí's eyes were drooping sleepily when the smooth-man who had brought the young woman to the strange-village came back with a dead-animal hanging across his shoulder. The smooth-man dropped the dead-beast on the ground at the door to the hut, and in its place threw Malaí over his shoulder. He carried her into the hut; it had a very narrow opening which Malaí and the man entered stooped over.

Malaí looked on the ground for a pile of leaves where she could lie down, but the floor was hard and clean. The man pointed to a net of fibers which was hanging up across the hut, fastened to two trunks. Malaí stood looking at it, without knowing what to do. The man swung the net, and since Malaí did not move from her place, he lifted up the girl by the waist and threw her into the hammock. Then, agile as a wild forest-animal, he climbed up himself and laid his smooth-body on top, almost suffocating Malaí.

Tira's father-man went to get the girl-woman. He opened the door of the hut, took his daughter from inside, and led her to the village entrance. The young women waited on the path, with many ornaments made of flowers and singing shells. They were laughing and making pretty sounds in their throats. Tira looked around suspiciously, thinking in her head about everybody fleeing from her, her mother-woman fleeing from her, Malaí fleeing from her. She did not know what to do. Then Ima came near the girl-woman and called Tira a young woman! She filled Tira's neck with pretty shell and flower necklaces, and laughed with her, and so did the others. Another woman smoothed Tira's hair with a fishbone. When Tira was all decorated and very pretty, they all went together into the village.

It was just like a feast!

Many fruits from trees were served in bowls, and there was an enormous spitted animal, all waiting for laughing mouths. There were good drinks which the old women had made. The women and the men wore colored ornaments and shells. Mother-woman waited for Tira at the door of the hut. Because the girl-woman-newly-young-woman was afraid of going in, her mother-woman called her, laughing, so the two of them could go in together.

Tira felt that it was very important to be a young woman, and became very happy. Everyone opened their faces to her. Everyone touched their fingers to Tira, and gave her ornaments, and brought her fruit, and held out gourds of good drinks to her lips. Tira saw everyone.

But Tira did not see Malaí.

The men who searched for Malaí reached a place where plants were so thick that the men could not see a path through which human-people could pass. They completely lost the signs of feet. The plants were strange, and the noises were strange.

The tired men wanted to go back. Karincai did not want to, but he looked around, lost, and the darkness was returning darker than before. The spirits-with-swollen-bellies, which were so full they almost dragged, became pale, and when they became pale their throats growled furiously like wild animals.

The wild-spirits in the sky announced that the men should return to the village and leave Malaí. Karincai could not fight against the wild-spirits. The other men were dying of fear, because men's courage and boldness can do nothing against the annoyance of the spirits. One does not play around with that!

So the men returned.

Chapter 7

The spirit which speaks thickly and the spirit which speaks thinly. The feast of the feather-men. The dance of the white-deer, and the fight of the men-beasts.

Malaí sat in the doorway of the hut and looked at everything, especially those human-people so different from her own human-people. One woman sitting in front of a hut made black drawings on the skin of another woman, using a sharpened tooth from a terrible-long-beast of the muddy-water. The first woman was drawing lovely rounded designs on the skin of the other woman. Malaí actually thought the designs were pretty, and sat watching, watching.

It seemed that something was going to happen, something very different from the things that had happened in those alike-days which Malaí had spent in the strange-village of the strange-people. New activity moved people here and there; they went and returned, talking and gesturing. They were doing something important in their own affairs.

Malaí looked and looked, but she did not understand anything. The talk of the strange-men rang in her ears, but left only a hole;

the words did not make images in Malaí's head. Sometimes the strange-man who was her owner, and who dragged Malaí to the high hammock every night, made signs which the young woman understood. But the strange-man did not bother to help Malaí understand many things, and the people of the village no longer found it interesting to be curious about her. So Malaí sat in a corner, watching. They no longer tied the young woman's feet and hands, since she really could not flee alone into the middle of the forest.

The old woman with the eyes lit from within was the one who always brought food to Malaí. The dry-woman laughed with her toothless mouth, and sat stooped down over her feet while Malaí ate. The old woman wanted to stay because no one paid any attention to her; she did not speak the strange-language either.

That day Malaí saw men going about their business from one side of the village to the other, talking and doing important things. She saw men tear up big-plants from the forest. They dragged a piece with thick bark into the village. The men sat and cut the sturdy trunk into pieces. Then they dug inside the trunk and threw away all the pith. Malaí did not understand what the men wanted to do with those hollow-disks.

When the disks of thick bark were empty inside, Malaí saw the men stretch over the two open sides the fine-skin of a beast, which they had let dry in the heat of the eye-of-fire. After it was ready, the men beat on the leather with a bone. From inside the trunk came a *boom!* as though the voice of a hoarse, fat spirit came out of a prison when the bone beat it.

Then the men took long thin reeds from tall tufts of plants; they cut the reeds and made little tubes with several holes in each one. When the holes in the tubes were ready, the men put the ends of the reeds in their mouths and blew, *toot.* . . . From inside each tube the thin, sharp voice of a funny spirit emerged. As the men covered one and another of the holes in the reed with their fingers, the voice stretched and shrank, becoming fatter and thinner, as though the spirit inside were changing shape.

The men blew on the reeds and covered the openings with their fingers. A variety of *toot-tweet* sounds came from within. . . . Malaí laughed, how she laughed at that playful spirit which escaped through the holes and had a voice which stretched and shrank, becoming fat and thin!

The men noticed foolish Malaí laughing there, but did not pay any more attention to her.

It must be very important to make openings in the reeds, *tweet, toot,* and to make rounded trunks, *boom!* They did it all very seriously. Only Malaí laughed at the fat voice and the thin voice of the spirits imprisoned inside.

The new-woman became tired of the spirits, and went to watch the women, who were scraping roots into bowls to prepare pudding. She saw the men go out with their spears to hunt beasts.

The men and women drew black lines on their smooth, dark skin; the men had straight lines next to one another, and the women made curved lines which formed designs. They all put on shell necklaces and many feathers from the colorful animals-that-fly. They even inserted feathers into their skin, in holes in their mouths, noses, and ears. Malaí laughed; it was funny to insert feathers into holes in the skin. Malaí laughed, but a shiver ran down her body and she made a face—that must hurt!

Malaí no longer had to remain seated at the edge of the hut; she could wander through the village as she wished. No one watched over Malaí, who had lost her fear of the strange-dark-smooth-men, and could now walk around inside the village without anyone noticing her.

Malaí looked at people and thought about things.

One woman, Uraúka, was always sitting in the doorway of her hut. Malaí thought about Uraúka because of the still expression on her face, which had an open smile and eyes flitting through the air, and because of her hands. Uraúka's hands moved gently over the roundness of her young woman's body, caressing the life which was growing within her.

The eye-of-fire was shrinking and settling itself behind the big-plants; it seemed to be ready to sleep. Tongues-of-fire, climbing up to bite the darkness and to spit out red on all sides, escaped from an enormous pile of branches which the men-boys had gathered together in the middle of the village. When the tongues were very tall, everybody came and sat in a circle around the fire.

The dark-men came with their black-straight lines next to one another, and colored feathers fastened to their bodies with the gum of a plant; colored feathers were glued to their heads, arms, and legs, and inserted into their mouths and noses. The women came with their dark-smooth bodies with black smooth-curved lines designed on them, and feathers and shells hanging around their necks. They came and sat in a circle around the fire. All of them, men and women, had their dark faces painted red, bright red. The bodies with black designs and red faces made the strange-men look terrifying, even more so because the tongues-of-fire danced their light on them, making grimacing expressions.

Some men dragged the strange hollow-trunks with the dry-skin of animals fastened on the ends to a place closer to the fire. They beat with the bones in their hands, making a *boom, boom, boom* come from within the trunks. The hoarse voice of the spirits came from within, speaking a loud *boom, boom, boom.*

The tongues-of-fire danced on the people, inventing even more terrible expressions on top of their terrifying red faces, lighting up and snuffing out eyes and mouths, as though the fire had taken hold in them and they emerged.

Other men took the thin, cut reeds and put them in their mouths. They blew on the spirits inside, which came out with voices, *toot, toot, toot.* The men's fingers covered up the voices of the spirits in the holes of the reeds, and they escaped through other holes. They stretched, they shrank, thinner and thicker.

And so it was: *Boom, boom, toot, boom, toot, boom, boom, toot, boom, toot.*

The men began to hit one hand on the other each time a *boom* or a *toot* came from the trunks and the reeds. The women also beat each time with one hand on the other.

Tweet, tweet, boom, boom, tweet, tweet, boom, boom—ever louder!

There was a time for the *boom* and a time for the *toot*. Malaí was already learning it, and she, too, could hit one hand on the other, just right, at the time for the *boom* and the time for the *toot*.

The old man of the village, with a terrible red face, stood up in his place. He picked up a bowl of fine dark-colored powder, which the women had prepared from the tiny seeds of plants. He took the bowl to each man and put a small tube in the nose of each one. He picked up a very small amount of the dark powder with his fingertips, and blew it inside the tube. The powder was very strong, and the men's heads became dizzy, and buzzed.

The women brought out a cup filled with a strong drink, which passed from one to another. They refilled the cup when it was empty. Even Malaí drank from the cup. Everybody drank, but only the men breathed the dark powder in their noses.

After a short time, the men and women got up and went to

stand one in front of another, with the women on one side and the men on the other. They began to jump on their legs and wave around their arms, accompanying the *boom*s and *toot*s, which were always the same and never stopped. It seemed that the voices of the spirits had been freed, and would never again stop.

The men then began to free their voices as well, imitating the howls of the wild animals, the voices of ferocious beasts. They jumped on their feet in front of the women, swaying from side to side and moving their arms, and the women responded with similar jumps, similar swaying, and similar waving of their arms.

Malaí thought that it was all funny; everything seemed good and right, just as when old Camiú had given the plant-that-laughs to the young woman.

The men, shouting and swaying, all changed places with the women, who, all shouting and swaying, in turn changed places with the men. Then the men pretended to attack the women, and the women pretended to flee from the men. The men held spears in their hands and acted as though they would stab the women. All of a sudden the women were no longer women, but the white-deer which the men always hunted in the forest around the village. The women–white-deer ran from the hunter-men and made antlers of their arms, tossing them in front of their lowered heads. They pawed at the ground with their feet, those women–white-deer which the men attacked with their spears.

Everything ended when the women–white-deer pretended to fall beneath the spears of the hunters.

Suddenly the *boom*s and *toot*s ended, and everything became quiet. Everybody stopped. From behind the tongues-of-fire which boiled and crackled in the middle of the village came a man entirely covered with feathers, with his head hidden in the middle of more feathers so only his eyes could be seen. Another man also came, all covered with the thick skin of a strange-animal which does not have legs and drags along in the dust, twisting its body from one side to the other.

Malaí had seen one such terrible animal killed. The dark-man who communicated with the village spirits had thrown a marvelous powder in the eyes of the beast. It had stood still, swaying with its body half erect. It had a sharp tongue which was divided and hung out completely. The beast's head was small and split up the middle to form a mouth. The tongue-of-fire which was the tongue of the beast had moved all around, and then suddenly stopped, hanging

out. The burning eyes of the beast suddenly were stopped, held
there, and the beast could do nothing against the dark-man, dom-
inator of spirits, who put an end to him with a spear.

The skin of a beast like that one, thick and full of surprising
designs, smooth and hairless, now covered the entire body of a
man.

In the middle of the village, very close to the fire, the two men
stopped in front of one another. The one with feathers and the one
with leather stared at one another with eyes which suddenly were
no longer theirs but were the eyes of the beasts which they pretended to be.

The man-of-leather lay down on the ground, and dragged himself through the dust, swaying his body from one side to the other,
slowly following the feather-man. The feather-man rapidly and
lightly fled from the man-of-leather. He jumped on his legs and
lifted up his arms full of feathers, shaking his arms just as the
beast-that-flies does.

The man-of-leather moves his body more rapidly, and slithers
ahead toward the feather-man, who jumps on his feet and, beating
his arms, escapes the man-of-leather. The tongues-of-fire beat on
the two men who fight, and become red, and dark yellow, luminous, shining, and then extinguished.

The man-of-leather lifts the trunk of his body from the ground.
Malaí, with her dizzy head, sees a long, red tongue as sharp as a
dart come from inside the mouth of the man-of-leather, who
sways back and forth when he comes closer to the feather-man.
The feather-man lets out a hoarse chirp and shakes his body and
beats his feathers. Malaí sees a beak on the red face of the
feather-man, she is sure she sees it!

The two fighting men are illuminated by tongues-of-fire which
become red and yellow, slender and thick, long and short. Malaí
swears that she sees two eyes burning in the face of the man-of-
leather, who is suddenly only a mouth which opens. The tongue is
there, red and pointed, moving and moving. The man-of-leather
is no longer a man; he is a beast. He jumps on top of the feather-
man, who shrieks a sharp chirp and opens his beak, because he
also is no longer a feather-man either. He is a beast, Malaí
swears, and she sees it! She sees!

The beast-of-leather jumps on the feather-beast, bites its neck,
and the two roll in the dust. The beast-of-leather wraps itself

around the neck of the feather-beast, tightening until the feathers stop beating and the beast falls quietly to the ground.

Malaí screams and everything is snuffed out.

When the young woman opened her eyes, she saw the men and women using their hands to tear apart pieces of a beast spitted in the middle of the fire. It smelled good!

The old woman who liked Malaí brought a piece for the young woman. The strange-people put on the meat of the beast an ash which felt strange on the tongue and tasted like the angry-water of Malaí's village. Malaí remembered the village and remembered Karincai, and water began to fall from her eyes. The water which ran from Malaí's eyes also had the taste of the angry-water, and the taste of the ash which the strange-men put on the meat of the beast. Malaí decided to eat the meat then, for the ash on it made it very good.

Malaí looked at the strange-men, who were all eating the meat of the beast, and at the women who were eating. The men buried their mouths in the meat and tore off pieces with their teeth until white, clean bones remained. Then they let out satisfied grunts from their throats, and wiped their hands on their smooth, shining stomachs. The red faces, their white teeth grinning, tore pieces of meat from the bones, and their eyes shone like sparks. The strange-men made Malaí afraid.

What if suddenly the beasts were finished and those grinning teeth in the red faces kept biting meat, tearing pieces from one another, and from Malaí?

It seemed that the white teeth in the red faces bit by themselves, without needing owners, and would continue to bite . . . to bite . . . to bite.

The tongues-of-fire lit up and then darkened the teeth in people's faces; they stretched and shrank, illuminated and snuffed out. The faces changed faces, and never kept still, and the teeth . . . oh, those teeth! Malaí was very afraid of the teeth which might go off alone grinning, chasing legs and arms!

The young woman relaxed a little when she saw the man-of-leather and the feather-man together, eating a big piece of the broiled beast, as if one of them had not eaten the other a little while before. Malaí thought about what it was which made her see things and made people turn into beasts. Because her head whirled as if it were going to leave her body at any moment, she had to hold it in place with her hands. Something made Malaí not be her proper self. The strange-men were not proper strange-men either. They looked like something else, sitting all around in the red-yellow of the fire.

The *boom*s and *toot*s had stopped; there were only white bones left around the hearth. The tongues shrank, and only a red sea of fire remained. There were men and women lying down in corners. For the first time Malaí saw them sleeping outside their huts; like the people of Malaí's village, they were very much afraid of the spirits of the dark.

Chapter 8

The feather-men have a name for each thing. Curved-poles and sharpened-rods which kill from afar. Of how the men fooled Cuaçu, *making themselves pass for what they were not.* Maeréboe, *the spirit which has no beginning or end. Of how little-beasts shiver the smooth skin of the day.* Kurixi, *who takes woman-prey on the day of* Koadzi.

Malaí did not know how long she had been in the strange-village. She could only understand the strange-people a little, and they could understand Malaí only a little.

One day the ugly-smooth-man who was Malaí's owner put around the young woman's neck a decoration made of small bluish fruits, and said it was *Ixiulani*. Malaí stroked the little bluish fruits with her fingers and repeated for her owner-man: "*Ixiulani*." The dark-smooth face painted with black lines no longer seemed to be quite so ugly.

"*Ixiulani, Ixiulani, Ixiulani*," Malaí repeated while she fondled the ornament clasped around her neck.

She went out of the hut to the clear day outside, so the other women could see Malaí's *Ixiulani* hanging on her neck. But the other women were very busy burning canes which grew in the still eyes-of-water, and sifting the ashes in a straw mat. That was how they got the salt to put on the meat they ate, because the strange-village was too far from the angry-water to take salt from it. Since the other women were busy burning canes and sifting the ashes, no one noticed the *Ixiulani* on Malaí's neck.

Malaí went to the hut where Uraúka sat in the doorway. Uraúka caressed the shining roundness of her body, which time was filling up, announcing life. Her face was still, and her eyes lost in the air, looking at things through her enchantment. The eyes in Uraúka's still face were so lost in enchantment that they did not see the *Ixiulani* on Malaí.

Malaí returned to the hut, sat down in the doorway with the *Ixiulani* wrapped around her fingers, and sat looking and looking. Malaí saw a small girl who went by with a completely green beast-with-feathers perched up on her head. Malaí thought it was very pretty-funny when the little girl extended her hand and the green beast-with-feathers jumped to the girl's hand to drink sweet-water from a small shell.

The girl laughed at Malaí, and Malaí laughed at the girl. The girl sat down close to Malaí with the green-beast which the young woman thought was pretty. Then the girl showed the green beast-that-flies to Malaí, and said *"Bolobedo,"* and the green-beast repeated, in a grating voice which seemed to be the spirit inside it: *"Bolobedo."* Malaí was amazed; she opened her mouth in astonishment, and then laughed.

"Bolobedo," said Malaí.

"Bolobedo," repeated the green-beast with the rasping voice of the spirit.

It was thus that Malaí began to realize that each thing had a name in the strange-village.

There were beasts-with-feathers all around. Men cut their wingtips to let them run free, or they tied them to the poles of the huts so they could climb on the roof. They called these beasts *Anikê,* and called the rounded eggs which the beasts laid in hidden corners *Anikexi*.

When Malaí showed these eggs to the girl (who was called Malika) and asked if they were to eat, the girl Malika made a contorted face. She pursed her mouth and said, "No, you do not eat that, it is terrible. You do eat the egg of *Kodoni*." Malaí asked what *Kodoni* was, and the little girl said it was the green hooked-face animal with a hard shell of glued-together-pieces, which Malai knew well. The little girl said, *"Kodonizi*, yes, is good in the mouth. Nobody eats *Anikexi!"*

"And do people eat *Anikê?"*

"No, nobody eats *Anikê*, either!"

"Then why are there so many *Anikê* running around in the village? Why does everybody have *Anikê?"*

"The *Anikê* spirit, of course. *Anikê* aren't for human-people. *Anikê* speaks with its own voice and does things only for its own self. That is why men do not eat *Anikê."*

Malaí nodded yes with her neck, very surprised.

The small girl made an important face, because she knew things and Malaí did not know anything! Quite full-of-air, she continued speaking: "Every beast-that-flies has a spirit inside it. The *Bolobedo* was a spirit which Malika received from her mother-woman to be a companion to Malika. The spirit-companion of Malika speaks! But the *Anikê* speaks differently. Do you want to see?"

The little girl said to the *Bolobedo:* "Malika!"

And the *Bolobedo* answered with the raspy voice of the spirit inside it: "Malika!"

Malaí was astonished indeed. In her village spirits did not live in the beast-that-flies. They lived inside shells, Malaí explained to the little girl.

"Shells don't walk and don't talk," said the girl importantly. "The beast-that-flies does! Malika has her own spirit-companion which speaks. Other people in the village also have their own spirit-companions."

Malaí nodded yes, she had seen them. The chief of the village (because this village did not have a Council of Old Men, but only one chief who told everyone what they ought to do) had a big beast with red feathers (Malaí had learned that the color red was called *Iwáulu*). The chief of the village had his *Iwáulu* beast-of-feathers which climbed on the chief's hut and was his spirit-companion. The chief of the village was called Aramoke, and was very important. When it was an important day, he wore on his head and on a great cloak only the feathers of the beast-that-flies. In the village there were always important days. Other men also had their own big beasts with red and blue feathers, or only blue or only red, climbing on their huts, and they also wore the

feathers of beasts when it was an important day. Malaí did not
know why, but they danced and danced until almost the end of the
darkness. Malaí had never seen men dance in the shell-mound
village. The strange-smooth-men were certainly very different!

Malaí looked at her own body and laughed, for now Malaí was
also all smooth. The women of the village had spread over
Malaí's body a paste made from the insides of a green-plant.
When the paste dried, the women had pulled it (with a scream of
pain from Malaí) and yanked it from Malaí's body. It came off
with all the hair stuck to it. In that way Malaí became smooth.

At first Malaí hid, because she felt very bad without hair on
her body. She sensed that she lacked something important; she
seemed to be doing something evil-wrong. Afterwards Malaí forgot about her smooth-body. Since no one thought it wrong for
Malaí to be smooth (they were all smooth), Malaí also became
used to her new-body.

Malaí looked at her smooth-body now and did not think it was
so bad. Now she had the *Ixiulani,* bluish and pretty, dancing
around her neck! Once Paleko, Malaí's owner-man, brought
sweet-honey (which he called *Nauekiezi*) in the bark of a tree for
Malaí to eat with meal. Malaí learned to give a name to each
thing. Now when she talked with Malika she did not need to use
so many signs.

On one beautiful awakening of the eye-of-fire, Paleko took
Malaí to gather honey in an open space in the middle of the
green-forest where there were big mounds of hardened earth almost the size of a man standing up. These were the homes of dark
small-beasts with transparent wings, which made their dwellings
by piling up dirt which became as hard as wood. It was full of
small rounded holes.

It was good to take *Nauekiezi* from these little beasties, because they did not bite the skin. There were others which made
their round homes in trees. They were dangerous because they bit
the skin very painfully, and came in swarms, going buzzzz, to
defend their homes.

The *Nauekiezi* was inside a storeroom, which was all hollowed
out with holes which were beautifully alike. After the *Nauekiezi*
was removed, the storeroom could be crushed and formed into a
thing called *Tabolá,* which was used by the people of the village
to fasten the feathers of the beast-that-flies to the skin of men.

People also made *Tabolá* from the milk which came out of the trees. *Tabolá* was very good and useful for many things, but Malaí really preferred the *Nauekiezi*.

Malaí and Paleko opened up the mounds of hard-dirt, which were the dwellings of the beast-with-wings, and took out the tasty stuff.

Paleko now kept Malaí occupied doing things, and time passed easily. Malaí sunk her mouth in the *Tabolá* full of *Nauekiezi*, and the sweet-honey ran down the sides of Malaí's face and on her fingers, which became golden like the rays of the eye-of-fire. Paleko licked Malaí's fingers and the sides of Malaí's mouth. Paleko's tongue collected the golden threads from Malaí's face, and Malaí laughed, she laughed with a shiver in it.

And so the time passed.

Malaí sometimes thought sadly about the old village and Karincai. But strange new things kept happening, and the curious Malaí forgot her sadness. It was thus when the eye-of-fire suddenly hid itself in the middle of the day and everything became dark when it was not time to be dark and when everything ought to be light. Malaí was frightened, but Paleko explained that an evil-witch had shot an arrow at the eye-of-fire, and that was why everything became dark. He said that the *Tijuu-Holo-Larari* would end, and the eye-of-fire would again shine in the sky above.

The strange-village was on the edge of a long, singing sweet-water, quite far from the angry-water. But the singing sweet-water had many fish all the time. It was actually easier to catch fish in the water-that-runs than in the angry-water, and the fish of the singing-water were not as dangerous as some of the fish in the angry-water. The waters were gentle and smooth, always running without raising walls of white foam. Besides this, there were many of the hooked-face animals (which they called *Kodoni),* which laid a large number of eggs (which they called *Kodonizi).*

Malaí was at the edge of the water-that-runs washing a dish when a trunk-that-floats came out from under a beautiful tall green-plant. A strong man holding an enormous long-pole with a cord tied on both tips stood on top of the trunk. He held a sharply pointed spear on the cord and stretched, stretched it so much that the long-pole bent over rounded and the cord almost doubled in half.

Then the standing man threw into the water a little fruit so red that its color shouted, calling attention to itself. He pointed the spear, which was held between the curved-pole and the bent cord, toward that fruit.

A fish came, wiggling its tail, swimming from one side to the other. It saw the *Iwáulu* fruit, and, *glub,* swallowed it.

At that moment the standing man let go of the cord which he had pulled with such force. The curved-pole straightened out, and the sharpened-rod went flying, *zap!* into the head of the fish. Then the man pulled the spear, which was bound with tree-fibers, and the fish came impaled on it.

This was the first time that Malaí saw the curved-rod which spits a spear into the air.

The first time that Malaí saw the curved-pole and sharpened-rod she did not imagine how dangerous they were. It was only on the hunt for white-deer that Malaí could see all the danger of such a powerful weapon.

The smooth-men burned an enormous space in the woods on the other bank of the water-that-runs. There they would spread out the seeds of the good-plant so they could eat them.

As they fled from the tongues-of-fire many beasts running from the heat and the smoke went to hide in another dense and protected part of the forest. They were the same beasts that Ua hunted, but now they had their own names, which the dark-men gave them. The big wild animal with dark fur and a big head with tufts of hair on it was for them the *Tapiira*. The yellow-spotted animal with wild-animal claws and terrible fangs was the *Iauráete*. But what they actually liked to hunt most was the meat of the beautiful-white-animals which had antlers fastened on top of their heads, and which they called *Cuaçu*.

The men had burned the green-forest on the bank of the water-that-runs, and there were no longer any tall-plants there which could hide a beast from the eyes of men. But the beasts needed to drink sweet-water, and they came carefully in herds to the edge of the water to drink together.

The *Cuaçu* came in herds to drink the water-that-runs before the eye-of-fire stretched out its luminous cloak and threw it over the earth, when you could hardly see the shape of things. There were many big *Cuaçu*, and also small ones, the *Cuaçu-mirim*. The smooth-men agreed to hunt the *Cuaçu*. Malaí saw that they prepared their short spears with very sharp points, dipping these points in mixtures of magic-plants that had a poisonous effect. Afterwards they fastened to the other end of the rods beautiful colored feathers from the beast-that-flies, so the companion-spirits would ensure the true flight of the dangerous weapons. Then the men did a strange thing: They tied the branches of green-plants around their bodies, on their arms, their legs, all over; even their heads were hidden in the middle òf the green-plants. Each man became his own green-plant.

Then, with the prepared rods in their hands, that band of men-plants went in the trunks-that-float to the other side of the water-that-runs, where they had burned the forest.

When they reached the other side, the green-men planted themselves at the edge of the water. They were quite perfect there, looking just like the plants which had been there before. They kept very quiet, as green-plants remain quiet, only moving their leaves softly, as real green-leaves gently stir.

Things were beginning to take on their own shapes, but were still colorless, when a herd of *Cuaçu*, very beautifully white with cumbersome antlers growing on the top of their heads, came, came.

The *Cuaçu* went without hesitation down to the edge of the water-that-runs; they had come there to slake their thirst. A *Cuaçu* raised its antlered head and looked around, and saw only green-plants which swayed gently, just as the *Cuaçu* were accustomed to see. The white-animal again lowered its antlered head and began to drink. The many *Cuaçu* drank calmly, without haste or alarm.

But the green-plants began to move very, very slowly. . . . The *Cuaçu* continued to slake their thirst.

The men-plants came closer and closer until they stopped. A curved-pole appeared in the midst of the green-branches, and in the center of it was a pointed one. The rounded one was stretched and stretched. . . . All at the same time each one pointed at a *Cuaçu*. The rounded one was stretched, stretched—*zap!* The men-plants let loose the cords and the sharpened-poles flew from all sides right to the very white mark. A *Cuaçu* fell to its knees very gently, fell smoothly to the front, while a red thread ran down its white skin. The heavy head fell to the side, sinking into the water-that runs. The red thread went down the white skin and spread out in the long-water, which was singing and running.

The men took off the green-branches and went to retrieve their prey.

When darkness fell, many *Cuaçu* would be prepared as food. First, however, the powerful man of the village who spoke with the spirits had to take the evil-spirits out of the *Cuaçu* so that the meat of the beast would not harm the men and women who would eat it.

The dead *Cuaçu* were all put on a woven mat in the middle of the village, to be offered to *Maeréboe*, the spirit which has no beginning or end, and should take away any evil from the meat. The old man who spoke with spirits was called Tumayana. He put his knees on the ground and squatted on his feet at the edge of the woven mat where the *Cuaçu* were.

A young man lit with a point of fire the clay-mouth of a small-length of cane with a hole in it, which he held in his own mouth. Coals formed inside the clay-mouth, and gave off smoke. The young man came close to Tumayana and put the long-cane into the mouth of the old man. The old man sucked on the long-cane with his mouth and smoke came out of the mouth-of-clay.

Afterwards Tumayana said that the smoke was for *Maeréboe*. He asked *Maeréboe* to come down next to him in the smoke, and to take away bad things and evil-spirits so nothing would happen to them, the sons of *Maeréboe*.

The head of the old man was almost hidden in the smoke. Suddenly he began to tremble, to tremble, to wave his arms, and to shake his head from one side to the other. Foam came out of Tumayana's mouth.

The men were all quiet around him. No sound was heard. Tumayana stopped, looked around with strange eyes, and was no longer Tumayana, but *Maeréboe* who had come down and taken over the body of the old man. The spirit without beginning or end was there in Tumayana's body.

The old man looked around at the men of the village, and said that he was there because he had been called on account of the *Cuaçu*, to take the evil-spirits from the *Cuaçu*.

Afterwards the old man again took the mouth-of-clay, blew inside it, and filled his mouth with smoke. Coming close to the mat, he doubled up his thin body, leaned against the open mouth of the prey, and blew the smoke into them so the evil-spirit would leave the bodies of the *Cuaçu*. Then the spirit-man as

signed the parts of the *Cuaçu* to the people of the village; he
showed the pieces and named the owners. Afterwards he put the
Cuaçu to cook in a big hearth which had been dug in the ground,
and was now full of burning embers. Tumayana ate the part belonging to *Maeréboe*.

Then Tumayana went into his hut to converse with the Great
Spirit until *Maeréboe* sent the old man away from his presence.
Tumayana made sure that nothing bad would happen to the peo-
ple, not injuries, illnesses, or hunger.

The hot day was so gentle over the village that it seemed you
could caress it, like the skin of an animal.

Malika, Malaí, and the other women had put the meat left over
from the *Cuaçu* in the sun, with ashes to salt it. Malika lifted her
eyes and sniffed. The warm air entered Malika, and she said to
Malaí that everything was very still, and that it had never been as
still as this. Malaí also felt that the unmoving leaves and the
women themselves sitting in the sun seemed like motionless
statues.

Everything was so quiet that it was a sudden shock when a
dark cloud of black-beasts with wings fell on the village. The
beasts were as big as fingers, and flew like blind people crashing
into everything.

The women let their tongues hang out in surprise and pleasure.

The men lit big fires of straw in the center of the village and
everyone, old and young, ran with gourds and pots after the
black-beasts, which singed their delicate transparent wings in the
flames, and fell.

When the cloud disappeared and the gourds and dishes were
full, men and boys laughing and talking a great deal put salty
ashes on their little-beasts and ate them with hungry mouths and
shining eyes. It was like a feast, like a shiver on the smooth skin
of the day which the people could caress like the skin of an animal.

Malaí and Paleko had finished eating a dishful when a
smooth-man arrived with a woman hanging over his shoulder like
dead prey, and threw Ima on the ground in the center of the village.

The village of the smooth-men had very few women. This
situation was a terrible punishment from the evil-spirits for those
men, because with few women the village could not grow, nor

other strong men be born to defend the people against attack by other peoples. That was why the smooth-men had decided to steal women from other villages. For a long time the smooth-men had done this; there were many other women in the village, before Malaí, who had come from outside. Little by little they had become like women of the village, learning their language and their way of doing things. When the women became old and their men sent them away, the men had to find others outside the village. It was Aramoke who took care of the old women who had no men of their own; he paid other men with weapons to hunt and fish for them. Only Aramoke had many women; the others had to content themselves with one. But when a woman became very old (some had already seen up to thirty risings of the water-that-runs), the man could send her away and arrange another new-woman for himself.

Paleko had gone to seek a woman from outside the village, and had discovered on the shore of the angry-water quite far from there a new shell-mound village which young men were building. Paleko watched the village for days and days until he took Malaí.

Kurixi, another young man from the strange-village, saw Malaí with Paleko, and wanted to do the same thing.

Kurixi left his village very early, after a darkness in which the sky had dropped a great, great deal of water. As he crossed the green-forest, Kurixi saw high up in the washed-out blue of the morning a colored-arch, which he knew was the shadow of a great-long-fish.

Kurixi wrinkled his forehead unhappily. The colored-arch, which they called *Koadzi*, was a bad sign. In fact, they said, a man who came close to it would die; the beast would make a *boom*, and the man would disappear. Kurixi looked at the bad-luck colored-arch, but did not stop. He went through places where the greenery had all the colors of green, walked for a long space-time, and when the eye-of-fire was high up overhead, came to the edge of the water near the shell-mound, where the great-blue-animal which they called *Pirauaçu* had been stuck.

Kurixi rapidly climbed up a thick-trunk. Hidden between green-branches, way up high, he sat watching what was happening in the village.

Ua braided a cord of tree-fibers so the trap would be strong, and said, "Ima, go get sweet-water from the stones for Ua."

Ima nodded yes with her head and picked up the water jug from the corner of the hut.

Ua said, "Ima, don't delay. Ua has thirst in his mouth."

Ima nodded yes with her head.

Ua continued braiding the cord for the trap with his quick big fingers. Everything of Ua's was big!

Ima put the jug on her shoulder and went out of the hut. The eye-of-fire was way up high, right in the waist of the day. Ima closed her eyes against the power of the light. She opened them slowly, but walked quickly, because an angry Ua made Ima afraid. Ima liked Ua, but was afraid, afraid of an enormous heavy hand which hit hard but caressed gently, gently (Ima felt a shiver), when Ua was not angry. But Ua's anger was worse than the scream of a wild animal or the roar of the angry-spirit up above in the sky when the gray-bodies were full!

Ima came to a singing water-from-the-stones, which came tumbling down from above and made a pool below. Ima went into the chilly water (how good it was!). The eye-of-fire was burning above, and the eye-of-water was chilly below (how wonderful!). Ima went in deeper and deeper, up to her waist, and it felt very good. The thick hair of Ima, which came smoothly down her body, floated in the water, the water rising up the girl's two fruits, which were bursting ripe. Ima forgot Ua's anger somewhat, and submerged her whole body in the sweet-water, coming out on the other side with water dripping down her whole body, and her whole self glowing in the water and in the fire which came down to her from the eye up above.

Kurixi, who was high up on a thick-trunk, between the branches, had enormous eyes which greedily swallowed those fruits bursting with ripeness. He had a dry tongue which drank ardently of the water that ran down, shining and dripping off the girl's body.

Now Ima, with the jug in her hand, was all golden and shining in the sun. She was a golden honeycomb dripping honey, and Kurixi was starving. The *Nauekiezi* which ran down the ripe honeycomb of the young woman was sweet in Kurixi's eyes. He forgot the colored-arch which brings bad luck, and lightly and agilely slid down the trunk.

Ima was bent over holding the jug to fill it with water. Kurixi came up behind her and grabbed Ima, but the girl thrashed out nimbly. Since she was wet she slipped out of Kurixi's hands and dove into the water. Kurixi plunged in behind her in a desperate fury, chased the young woman, and grabbed her by the legs. Ima kicked Kurixi hard in the mouth, which opened up a gap that dripped *Iwáulu*. Kurixi did not pay attention, but grabbed the young woman by the hair and pulled the great-female-fish out of the water, while she kicked and flailed her arms like a madwoman. Kurixi had to hit Ima several times with his hand for her to stop. He hit her hard, and Ima fell with a limp body at Kurixi's feet.

The surprised smooth-man leaned over and listened to the mouth of the young woman; she was breathing. Kurixi then became more calm and threw Ima over his shoulder. Her long smooth-wet hair fell to the other side, down Kurixi's back like a cloak. The woman-prey swayed her arms like a dead-person, and did not see the long path which Kurixi walked, full of greens of all colors, and of other beauties which a laughing spirit had put there for men to enjoy.

Kurixi walked for a long time with his still-sleeping woman-prey hanging over his shoulder. The day was hot and gentle; it seemed that you could caress it, like the skin of an animal, when Kurixi stepped into the village. When he came into the middle, he threw the young woman on the ground.

All the men sitting in the middle of the village, around the great fire where they cooked their prey, heard what Kurixi told. They heard of the new village built next to the enormous-blue-animal which they called *Pirauaçu*. They heard with big, open ears what the men of the village of the angry-water were like with hair over their entire bodies. Some of the smooth-dark-men twisted their noses in their faces in a gesture of dislike for the ugliness of the men-with-hair—but the men-with-hair had many young women.

The smooth-men feared the greatest punishment which the spirits could send to a brave people, as they thought themselves to be: to pass on to the abode of the spirits without leaving behind the perpetuation of their tribe. This fear had tormented the men of the village for many risings of the water-that-runs, and now they saw a way to solve their problem.

Two men had already managed successfully to steal women from the men-with-hair, without being seen, and without their knowing who had taken the prisoners. They had been very lucky not to be seen. Now stealing women had to be a well-prepared plan, no longer up to each man, but the business of everybody in the village and, ultimately, the responsibility of Aramoke. Now it was he who had to make a decision and think of a good idea to ensure the perpetuation of the brave men and of their tribe.

Chapter 9

The good idea of Aramoke. Of how stories enter the big-ear of Aramoke. Of the men-of-straw and their ways. Of how the good idea of Aramoke became even better. The spirit-of-wood which steals women. The fear-that-drives.

Ua finished fixing the trap. He waited and waited, and began to get angry. Ima was being disobedient. Ima must be doing nothing along the trail, instead of bringing a jug of sweet-water to Ua.

Ua became more and more angry, hurling out shouts of annoyance. He went out of the hut with his mind made up and his arms ready to punish Ima.

Ua walked to the stones which formed a pool full of water, which fell rolling down from the rocks above. Ua looked and looked, but saw nothing until he saw Ima's gourd fallen on the ground, but no Ima. Ua did not understand what had happened. For that reason he returned, still angry, expecting to meet Ima doing nothing along the path. He went with his mind made up and his arms ready to punish the stubborn woman.

He went into the village with a frowning face, and spoke angrily with the other men, asking if they had seen Ima. The other

men came near and surrounded Ua. Their faces were also frowning, but for another reason. Ua told what had happened; the other
men listened to Ua's words, and became worried.

It was Karincai who said that the way of Ima not being there
anymore was much like the way with Malaí.

Then Ua hit himself in the head with his closed hand, for now
he understood.

All the men were upset. Strange-people, whom no one had
ever seen or even knew about, were wandering around near the
village and stealing women. There was now no doubt. The men
of the shell-mound had themselves done that to other men from
other villages. The women must no longer leave the sight of the
men. That was difficult, because the men still had ahead of them
a great deal of hard work to do in the angry-waters. There were
no old-old men in the new shell-mound to stay with big-eyes,
taking care of things. Consequently, the young men decided that
they would go out to do their work in two halves; one group
would stay to watch while the other did what had to be done.

And so it was.

Kurixi had been bitten several times, but he was very pleased
with the new-woman. Soon he asked the other women of the
village to spread *Tabolá* over Ima's body and to pull hard, yank-
ing off those ugly hairs so the woman would become smooth and
more to Kurixi's liking.

But Ima was not Malaí, and she kicked, hit out with her arms,
and shouted loudly, and she had to be tied up securely (between
roars) so that her ugly hairs could be pulled off. Her body did not
become pretty and smooth like Malaí's, because it remained covered with purple bruised spots and red scratches. The other
women also ended up with purple spots and red scratches, and
they finally fled from Ima, who was more fierce than a beast.

Kurixi had a new-woman, but he could not get close to her.
Ima finally calmed down a little bit when she saw Malaí. But
when she understood that neither she nor Malaí would ever again
return to the shell-mound, that she would no longer belong to Ua,
and that the man-owner of Ima was now that horrible-dark-
smooth small-man with his nude chest covered with black marks,
(unlike Ua's big strong hairy chest), then Ima roared even more
loudly and shoved Malaí, who was no longer Malaí but a smooth-
hairless-woman. Afterwards Ima hid her face in her arms so she

could not see Ima, who was no longer Ima but a smooth-hairless-woman.

The other women laughed from afar at Ima's desperation, but they soon paid no more attention. Such things could not engage the women's attention for much time. Even Malaí tired of hearing Ima's shouts, and went away. At last Ima herself tired of her shouts, and she slept with her body rolled up in a ball, curled up on the hard clean ground in a corner of Kurixi's hut.

Kurixi slept in his high hammock, swinging happily up above, looking down at his new-woman, who was now very angry but would end up being gentle.

Aramoke spoke of his idea to the other smooth-men of the village. He went from hut to hut to see each of them, because the smooth-men did not form a Great Council. They all thought his idea was good.

"After all, no one has ever seen dark-men in the shell-mound village. Who knows, maybe this way we could steal women without having to fight and sacrifice young men."

The smooth-men liked to fight, but not when their tribe was in danger of ending because they had few women and almost no children. If they could use that idea to bring back women, so much the better, even if it took time, and even if they could bring only a few women back at a time. If the hairy-men did not know who took their women, they could not fight in revenge or go after the women to bring them back.

Aramoke's idea was good, and very, very clever.

The smooth-men of the village began to prepare for the great event.

Aramoke painted his body as though for a great feast and wore the feathers of the animal which was his spirit-companion, to show that he was the most important man in his village. Some of the other men also painted themselves and wore feathers which indicated, in their way, that they were messengers.

After they were ready, they filled a net with stones which had been taken from a great mountain near the water-that-runs, and big red and blue feathers from beasts-that-fly which, they knew, the men of the shell-mound did not have in their village or close to it.

A group of men followed Aramoke, who wore beautiful feathers (which indicated, in their way of dressing, that he was the chief) and had no weapon to attack or frighten the men of the other village. The various men who went with him did not carry weapons of attack either.

Farther back, other men followed with hidden sharpened-rods stuck into braided tubes hanging down their backs and fastened to their chests with beautiful pieces of painted tree-fiber, which looked like decorations. The only parts of the rods which could be seen outside the tubes were beautifully colored feathers. These men held in their hands the enormous bows which the men of the shell-mound did not know. The bows had no points, or anything which was frightening. Nothing made them look like weapons; they looked more like pretty, decorated adornments. These men followed the others at a discreet distance.

When the painted smooth-men, full of colored feathers and without any weapons of attack, arrived ceremoniously and stepped out onto the great expanse of white-sand at the edge of the angry-water, the men of the shell-mound who were on guard got their spears ready, and waited.

Aramoke raised his arms in a wide gesture, and bared his strong chest. The other men put on the ground, there in the distance, the stones and feathers which they had brought.

Then they stepped back.

The other men who carried sharpened-sticks and curved-sticks stayed well behind. They looked as decorated, as festive, and as unarmed as the first men. None of them seemed to pose a threat.

The men guarding the shell-mound came forward, looking at the stones which were unlike any they already had. They were already well polished and useful, strong enough to cut down big-trunks, and could be sharpened to make good spears. They also looked at the pretty-pretty enormous feathers taken from beasts-that-fly which they did not know, like those which decorated the smooth-men so beautifully.

The guard-men talked among themselves, and talked, and finally went to consult Kotia–Kotiatí in their huts in the middle of the village. Aramoke waited at a distance, full of important dignity, with his men around him.

Kotia–Kotiatí came, nodded yes to Aramoke, and ordered some pretty shells, fishbones, and fresh fish which they had caught in the angry-water to be brought for Aramoke to choose. Aramoke showed interest in the spines, the thin-pointed bones of the fish from the angry-water, which he thought could be used as sharpened-points for the rods-that-kill-from-a-distance. He also pointed at some pretty shells which he liked a great deal, and which were difficult for a village in the middle of the green-forest to obtain.

Kotia—Kotiatí nodded yes again, and the smooth-men with feathers went away; the men of the shell-mound returned to their village.

Thus, when Aramoke and his people came to the long-white-sand another time, the guards of the shell-mound were no longer suspicious or afraid of those colorful men with feathers and without weapons. In this way trade, which was profitable for both sides, began.

It was not spines and shells which Aramoke's men needed, however. Aramoke's idea was one with a delayed result. He had to bring the men of the shell-mound out of their village and away from guarding the women. He had to distract them for a time while a group of other men took away the women. It was important that the shell-mound men not distrust Aramoke and his smooth-companions decorated with feathers.

That way a fight would not be necessary, for the robbed men would not know them, or know whom to fight.

Kurixi now thought that the colored-arch of *Koadzi* on high had been a bad sign, telling him not to steal the woman from the shell-mound. Kurixi's shins were purple, and although he had taken a stick and beaten on the woman a great deal to make her become gentle, Ima became even more furious. Kurixi had not been able to use his woman, who was angry-wild, and who bit with her teeth and shoved with her feet each time he came near.

Malaí brought food and water to Ima, but she remained a beast curled up in a ball in the corner of the hut. Malaí spoke to her rationally, but Ima, who was very stubborn, did not want to accept her logic: "That small-smooth-man? No!" Ima did not want to believe that the strange-village was forever.

Malaí talked about new and different things in the village to interest Ima, and used her fingers to untangle the thick hair of the young woman, who stayed forgotten in a corner, paying attention to nothing.

After the eye-of-fire closed up above and things were hidden from view, there came the dark-time which the smooth-men (who had a name for each thing) called *Pituna*.

When *Pituna* came, Malaí dragged Ima out of the hut and began to talk about things to distract the other woman.

"There high in the *Pituna*," said Malaí, pointing up, "shine tiny lights that Paleko showed Malaí. Those lights, says Paleko, are a flock of *Bolobedos* flying high in the *Pituna*. Those other lights"—Malaí pointed—"are an enormous flat dark fish, with a long tail and wide arms which look like the wings of the beast-that-flies. Malaí never saw these fish in the angry-water, but Karincai said they slap their tails and swim by swinging their arm-wings a great deal."

Afterwards Malaí began to make beautiful sounds in her throat, singing and hitting her hands as the men did during their dances. Ima looked at Malaí and thought that that-smooth-woman was no longer Malaí. Opening a big-mouth in tiredness, she went into the hut and rolled herself up in the corner to sleep. Ima's body could not get comfortable on the smooth-hard ground. She looked at the net hanging up high, held it with her hands, and swung it gently. Then she climbed onto the net, stretched out her body, and thought it felt very good. Ima soon turned off the ideas in her head, and rolled deeply, like a stone, into herself.

A great time-space of distance away, well within the green-forest, by trails which required a time in which *Pituna* and the eye-of-fire follow one another very, very often, was the village of the men-of-straw. Camina and Maitá, two old women who had already lived for their men and who now lived to tell their stories, had come from there.

The men all knew the stories Camina and Maitá told about the men-of-straw, and no longer paid attention. But the old women were always repeating stories about their tribe, speaking alone, mashing the words in their shriveled mouths, even when no one listened to them.

It was Aramoke who took care of the old women who had no masters, and he paid men to hunt and fish for those women. That was his responsibility. The women who lost their men in battle were also his responsiblity, if they did not have male relatives.

Aramoke braided his bow, and listened without hearing. Suddenly the chewed words of the old women dug out a hollow-space in the chief-man's ear, and some of the words entered it:

"It was a dance for men only, not women. No one saw the face of whoever's face it was, because it had painted wood on top of it, and no one saw the body of whoever's body it was, because it had straw all around, down to the ground."

Aramoke pointed his ear toward the old women, and decided to listen to the story.

"The clothing always remained guarded in the house-of-sound. It was hung up, and the faces of wood painted to hide the faces of the men were also hung up. Women did not go into the house-of-sound."

"When *Pituna* arrived, the men of the village went into the house-of-sound and came out with faces of wood and bodies of straw, so no one knew which man was which."

"Then they began to dance. They danced, and yelled the shouts of angry wild animals. Then they banged on each hut, and everybody had to give food and drink to the men-of-straw. It was said that they were spirits when they were that way."

"In their hands they shook the head bones of *Macacaitá*, with stones inside and feathers of beasts fastened to the ends. The bones went *shikee, shikee, shikee* when they were shaken, and were called *Ualú*. The men danced, swaying their straw bodies and shaking the *Ualú* at the same time."

Aramoke began to think about many men with faces of painted wood and strands of straw hanging all around their bodies down to the ground, men with faces which hid their faces and with straw bodies which hid their bodies. No one would ever know who such men were. They would only know that they were men-of-straw, and if they were men-of-straw, they were not men-of-feathers!

Aramoke was working out an idea better and better in his thoughts, and no longer listened to the story of the old women. In his head he told his own story, and it made Aramoke's face open wide and his tongue hang out in pleasure.

Aramoke put down the braid he was working on for his bow, and went from hut to hut to tell the smooth-men the new thought-idea he had imagined.

The men all thought it was a very good plan. The men-of-straw lived very, very far away, and the men of the shell-mound probably knew nothing about them. The feather-men would make clothing of fibers-of-straw, and faces of painted wood. Afterwards, some of the men would dress up in this attire, and go with

very quiet steps through the densest part of the forest to the village of the shell-mound.

A time would come for the men-of-straw to go into the shell-
mound. This was Aramoke's idea, which he was braiding slowly,
just as he carefully braided the end of his bow.

The smooth-men spent days and days carving very frightening
faces into pieces of wood. The faces were then painted with
Iwáulu, so they took on a very evil and angry appearance.

When everything was ready, Aramoke painted his body as for
a great feast, and put on the feathers which showed that he was
the chief. He ordered a net to be filled with stones which were
streaked dark and light. They were covered with shining points,
which looked like tiny eyes-of-fire. The hairy-men had never seen
stones like that. He also ordered nets filled with colorful feathers
for trade: There were enormous blue and red feathers, the green
feathers of the *Bolobedo,* some pretty light blue ones, and yellow
ones (which had never before been seen at the shell-mound).

Other men put on beautiful feathers and painted their bodies.
A pretty piece of fiber-from-a-tree on each man's chest secured a
braided tube which hung down his back. Only beautiful colored
feathers could be seen above the tube. The men of the shell-
mound were already accustomed to these decorations on the men-
of-feathers. They carried no weapons of attack in their hands.
Each man held only a beautiful curved-piece of wood, without
points, which was covered with a braid with pretty designs, and
was tied on both sides with a cord.

Thus the men-of-feathers went ahead to the beach of the shell-
mound.

On the beach near the village some men threw their nets and
spears into the trunks-that-float. Karincai and other men went
onto the rocks where their dives could bring back oysters, mussels, and other shells to the village.

A few men stayed on guard: Kotia Kotiatí, and some others
with their weapons. Gradually fewer men were staying, for time
was passing and nothing more had happened.

The men went away on the trunks-that-float. The noise of the
white foam beat repeatedly on the quiet white of the great-sand
which stretched beyond view. In the village the women began
their work as they did every day. Ua left for the green-forest with
his spear. Some other men stayed around doing nothing, stretch-

ing their arms and stretching their legs, and opening big-mouths
of laziness. The day was warm and still, and the noise of the
white foam repeated itself, always-always repeated itself, beating
on the quiet white of the great-sand which was so wide it
stretched beyond view.

The sight of the guard-men was lost lazily against the expanse
of the white-sand and the expanse of the angry-water. The eye-of-
fire pushed the sight of the guard-men toward the dark inside
themselves, and their sight was extinguished.

When the sight of one guard-man blinked its eye, he saw, far
off, the men-of-feathers arriving.

The guard-man's arms and legs grew springs, popped him up
quickly, and he went to warn everyone. The other men woke up
from their laziness and showed alert faces. Kotia and Kotiatí went
out of their huts. They all went to the great-white-sand to meet the
men-of-feathers, because the men-of-feathers never entered the
village. Whenever they traded, they waited far off for the men of
the shell-mound to come to them, in the middle of the beach
where the air was empty behind each one of them, and the eyes of
one group could watch the empty space behind the back of the
other. (Men are always distrustful. They are always distrustful
because they know, with their own treacherous thoughts, that
other men are like them.)

The feather-men waited far from the village, and the shell-
mound men went to deal with them, carrying shells and fishbones
to trade, as they always did.

Aramoke opened his arms and bared his wide, dignified chest.
Kotia–Kotiatí received Aramoke like an old acquaintance. The
feather-men, colorful, festive, and without weapons, were themselves big colorful birds in the morning, without surprises or
dangers.

The feather-men put down on the ground the net filled with
stones which were striped dark and light and had brilliant points
on them, and nets full of beautiful feathers: blue and red, green
and light blue, and yellow, many shades of yellow, pretty feathers
with colors the shell-mound men had never seen before!

The shell-mound men looked, with eyes big and enchanted by
the colorful beauty spread out on the ground, and talked among
themselves. In turn they showed their most beautiful shells and
their strongest and sharpest spines. But Aramoke said no with his
head.

The shell-mound men, enchanted by the lively colors of the beautiful feathers and the strange brilliance and stripes on the stones, put more shells on the trading pile, and doubled the number of bones, for they wanted the green feathers of the *Bolobedo* (did green feathers really exist?) and the light blue ones which were the color of the space up above (did they exist?). The men picked them up in their fingers and brushed them, to see if the color would go away. There were large yellow feathers the color of the eye-of-fire, some darker and some lighter, all the colors that the eye-of-fire could become. And there were the stones with little reflections coming from them.

Aramoke took his time deciding, and the time passed. The shell-mound men, however, did not notice the time pass.

They had their backs to the village, and Aramoke's men watched the open space at their backs. The shell-mound men also watched the space behind Aramoke's men, and noticed nothing strange. The time passed.

Suddenly the feather-men who watched the space made a signal to Aramoke. Aramoke changed his thinking, and nodded yes with his head. He gave all the beautiful feathers in trade for the same shells and bones to which he had said no previously.

The shell-mound men were very pleased and began to gather together their feathers, without hurry. But now the feather-men were suddenly in a great hurry. They rapidly gathered together the shells and the bones, and left without waiting for the men of the village to gather the feathers into the nets. And the feathers had been all spread out!

When the men finished gathering all the feathers there was no more sign on the great-white-sand of Aramoke and his men.

When the shell-mound men had gone to meet with the feather-men far off on the white-sand, Kotia–Kotiatí went with them. They all went, except Ua who had gone with his spear into the green-forest to search for wild beasts.

The women went about their work as they did every day.

Tira, the young-woman–girl, separated the fibers of the vegetable-plants from the edge-of-the-water and stretched the fibers out, joining some together. The strips of fibers were becoming long, lo-o-o-ong, and she was wrapping-ing-ing them around a piece of bone.

Other women sitting in a circle sharpened the men's tools, scraping and scraping; they used sand and water, and scraped and scraped. They made a constant noise which they mixed with laughter and talk. They were so busy with their scraping, laughing, and talking that they did not hear the branches of the tall-plants breaking around the village and did not notice the strange piles of straw which came out from behind the greenery, and came closer, and closer...

Tira, the young-woman-girl who was spinning the fibers, suddenly raised her head. She saw (with an icy-coldness running down the middle-thread of her back), she saw (with her eyes opening up enormously wide and almost jumping out in dread), she saw (with a hoarse shout which almost suffocated her, because it was caught in her throat), she saw the red and hideous face of a wood-spirit with grinning teeth and enormous evil eyes, she saw a horrible face of wood which had no body but just an enormous beard of straw which it dragged and dragged, coming closer and closer...

The other women heard her muffled shout and raised their faces from their work. They saw (with an icy-cold running down each back like a sliding worm), they saw (with enormous terrified eyes), they saw (with sharp screams which did not have enough power or time to come out entirely from inside them), they saw many horrible men-of-straw with horrendous painted faces of wood. They must be spirits-of-evil, they must be! The women were glued to the ground by fear and shock. They screamed no more; their mouths were stuck open. The men-of-straw came dragging, dragging, and rapidly grabbed all the women who were sitting there outside the huts. The ones who screamed received heavy blows and fell head-first like dead-game. It happened so quickly that in an instant the men-of-straw were again dragging along into the forest and everything was finished.

Ua was in the middle of the forest, hidden behind some tall-plants, his spear ready to attack. A small dead-animal fastened by a thick-thread was the trap, waiting for the fierce-beast which Ua knew (he sensed the odor in his wrinkled nose) was close by.

Ua did not make a sound; he sat very quietly, since the fierce-beast distrusts any strange noise. But the smell of the dead animal was a strong lure, and Ua waited, knowing that.

Ua was waiting quietly when the rapid noise of the stepping of many-feet came from afar, coming closer and sounding like a troop of big-animals. Ua thought about the big furry beasts which walked imitating men, with their long arms hanging down. The noise was nearer and Ua flattened himself behind a pile of leaves. The band came closer and closer and passed through an open-space quite close to Ua.

It was then that he saw. The young man, with his eyes full of shock, saw an incredible thing. Men-of-straw, with faces of wood, horrible faces with grinning teeth (and there were many), went past carrying on their shoulders women (women from the shell-mound), many women, all of them hanging down, swinging their heads and their stretched-out arms like dead-game. Ua saw, but it could not be true; Ua's eyes must be imagining things that were not. Faces-of-wood dragging beards-of-straw passed by Ua and disappeared into the thickets. The noise disappeared. Ua was alone, and it took some time for him to rub his eyes and come to an understanding of what had happened.

Then Ua thought. He imagined in his head Ima being carried like dead-game by a face of wood dragging a beard-of-straw, and the water jug fallen on the ground. He imagined farther back, to Malaí being dragged by a man-of-straw with a horrible face-of-wood, and the bowl of fish strewn on the ground.

Ua did not think about spirits. Ua knew they were men, men from some far-off village stealing women from the shell-mound, and carrying them away to some place the shell-mound men did not know.

Then Ua quickly ran back to the village on the beach.

The men of the shell-mound gathered together the colorful pretty-feathers, and gathered the stones which were striped dark and light, with brilliant points. When they finished getting every-thing together there was no more sign of Aramoke and his men on the great white sand. They went back, very satisfied with their beautiful trade acquisitions.

They had scarcely entered the village when the empty-silence stabbed the men right in the place of their mistrust. The women's work was there on the ground, quiet (the threads they joined, the stones they smoothed). The men could not fit the size of their shock inside themselves.

"Where are all the women?"

Some older women and some young women with children hanging on them hurried out of the huts. They all had big-astonished eyes in their faces. After they stood for a moment without talking, they all loosed their tongues at the same time.

They talked about a thing beyond understanding, of spirits which dragged themselves, of faces-of-horror with grinning-teeth and beards-of-straw. The men of the shell-mound did not understand anything.

Ua came running into the village and told about the men-of-straw.

Then everyone understood.

The men-of-straw were unknown men from some distant village who had carried off the women belonging to the men of the shell-mound.

Kotia asked what they had looked like, but the men-of-straw had hid their likenesses under bodies of straw, as they hid their faces inside horrendous faces of painted wood. No one knew where to find such men.

Kotiatí thought that the feather-men might know where the men-of-straw were, but no one knew, either, where the feather-men lived.

The men of the shell-mound did not know what to do, but they had to search for the women. They could not sit there waiting; they would never be safe again.

So many men-of-straw must have left traces, like a pack of wild animals, no matter how careful and intelligent they had been. There were many of them (Ua had said), and they were in a hurry.

Kotia spoke. They could not wait for the other men to come back from the angry-waters. They had to follow the wooden-faces. Who knows, maybe they would be able to catch them.

Kotia, Kotiatí, and some men well armed with their spears then left, following the faint traces left by the straw-men. They made bigger signs so the other men from the trunks-that-float could follow after them. Ua stayed, guarding the new village alone. Ua thought that the new village had brought a bad fate to the men. He thought about the big-blue-animal being attacked by the ferocious-fish, and thought about Manaú without his good-leg going away to the dwelling of the shell-spirits. . . .

Ua wondered whether the men had occupied (who knows?) the dwelling of spirits, which had advised the men to go away, but the men had not understood and were now being destroyed.

Ua was alone in the middle of the village, looking far off at the angry-water, waiting for the return of the trunks-that-float.

* * *

As soon as the straw-men knew that they were far from the
shell-mound, they threw the sleeping women on the leaf-covered
ground. They took off their wooden-faces and beards-of-straw,
and hid them in the middle of a thicket where no one would ever
see them.

The dark-smooth-men appeared with their own faces.

Ikanoa, a smooth-man, led the group. Ikanoa said, "The men
can rest. . . ."

The heavy woman-game spread out on the ground now woke
up alive. Shocked, with their heads aching from the blows, they
were silent-beasts with terror in their eyes.

The awake women now knew that the straw-spirits with horrible faces of painted wood were human-people, and the fear of the
women changed.

The men had run a great deal, and their swollen tongues in dry
mouths needed sweet-water. Ikanoa and his men sniffed the air
around them with wrinkled noses, and the smell of sweet-water
came, telling them where they should find a still-eye of water that
was good to drink.

Ikanoa and the men pushed through the walls of green-plants,
surprising the beasts which were drinking. They lay down at the
edge of the sweet-eye, putting their mouths into the water and
sucking it up in their throats with fat *glug-glugs*.

The women of the shell-mound now lost their aspect of silent-
beasts, and their fears again changed. The women's fear became
urgent and suddenly awoke strength within them, a strength of
cleverness which told them to flee, a strength of desperation
which forced them to run away, without considering the danger. It
was a fear like that of a small-beast when Ua fastened it in a trap
and the beast, in a panic, pulled and pulled its body, even though
its foot was caught and could not be released. The drive to flee
was immense, and the beast bit its captured foot, bit with frenzied
teeth tearing at the flesh, breaking the bones, until the captured
foot was separated from the free rest of its body. When Ua came
he found only the bloody foot of the little-beast in the quiet trap,
telling a story of desperation and the strength of the fear-that-
drives.

The women of the shell-mound now felt that same strength
and desperation of the fear-that-drives, and they decided to take

advantage of the men's rest to flee, running any way they could, to flee!

The women got up, some hanging on the others, and, without looking behind their heads, they ran off, their feet stepping on the ground over branches, thorns, and stones (they did not feel them). Their feet were now on their own; the women no longer controlled them. The fear-that-drives carried the women, even if their feet would have stayed.

The men slaked their thirst with fat *glug-glug*s and returned with water dripping from their faces and chests. When they arrived where the woman-game had been lying, they understood that they had fled. The men took up their weapons and, now without the straw-clothes tripping them up, they ran after the women.

The women ran, tracing the footsteps the men had made earlier. Their feet were already losing pieces of skin when the men, who ran more and knew the trail, arrived and closed off the path.

Ikanoa grabbed one woman and hit her head with such force that bones broke and the woman's head dangled from her shoulder. Ikanoa threw the woman into the forest and grabbed another, who hit and scratched the chest of the smooth-man, leaving deep tracks of each finger of her hand. Ikanoa ground his teeth furiously in his anger, and hit the woman with a pointed-stone. He hit her until the woman's face became a red mass which still gasped for air with an ugly big-noise. Another man came and stuck his spear into the chest of the wounded animal-person, which stopped the noise.

The man called Makuré ran after another woman, who tripped, got up and ran, and tripped again. Makuré held the woman by her hair. The woman-beast pulled at the hair captured in the trap, pulled and pulled. The man's hand held on tightly. The woman pulled desperately. The hand-trap tightened more and more. The woman pulled with a jerk, left behind the hair from her head, and fled with the shrieks of a wild beast. Makuré looked at the hair which remained in his hand-trap, with pieces of skin hanging fastened to it.

The men continued running, grabbing women, and hitting, and hitting. A few women (some who remained quiet) were thrown over shoulders and carried away again. Those who struggled and kicked were run through with spears and hit with sharp stones.

Finally everything was quiet.

The smooth-men carried the ones who survived, and left for their village.

Chapter 10

The story of Uraúka and the seed-of-man. The story of Dioraná, the woman who fled. What the shell-mound men know and Chief Aramoke does not know. The fight. How Aramoke saw the colors of Koadzi explode. Of how Karincai saw the bird-without-wings fly.

The village of the smooth-men was quiet and still. Some men had gone off decorated with feathers, other men had left wearing strange-clothing of straw and ugly-faces of wood. The women had remained in the village with their everyday work. The day was warm and slow, and the companion-beasts twittered on the roofs of the huts.

The old men busied themselves behind the houses of the village, digging into the earth with poles, making little holes like fingers, and putting seed-grains in them. The old women kneaded dough in containers of beautifully colored clay. There were yellow, red, black, and greenish bowls, for they were able to find clay of various colors in different places. The containers were covered with a thin layer of material which came from inside the husk of plants which they knew, and which made the containers shine like water.

Not a sound was awake in the village of the smooth-men; everything was gentle and still. Only Uraúka (the woman with the enormous-belly, supported by a band of coarse fabric) walked restlessly, from one side to the other, from one side to the other.

Uraúka's mother-woman waited without saying anything. Only the mother-woman's eyes in her closed face followed Uraúka fiercely, from one side to the other, from one side to the other.

The enormous-belly of the smooth-woman shook inside. Life was going to awaken, she felt, human-life!

The master-man of the swollen-woman was far away, with Aramoke and his men. But this was not important. The new human-life within Uraúka was only her concern, until it set itself free. Uraúka's mother had brought herbs and prepared a drink which would help free Uraúka's fat-belly of its great burden. The young woman swallowed the drink which her mother-woman prepared.

Uraúka walked and walked. She stopped occasionally, emitting a groan, feeling a sharp pain which was born in her back and ran to the front. The attentive eyes in the dry old face of the mother-woman followed Uraúka here and there. They seemed to be counting the time, here and there.

The time began to go more quickly with the sharp pain which cut the body of the smooth-woman in two parts even more often. The eyes of the mother-woman followed more rapidly, and Uraúka's groans were repeated more often, here and there, inside the village. Then the round-belly tore deep inside. The young woman stooped down on her feet, and with a torn scream she let a small form of red, weak flesh fall onto a pile of leaves on the ground.

The mother-woman took the small form which was still caught hanging between Uraúka's legs on a long red gut, tightened the gut, twisted it with her hands, tied it well with a fiber, and cut it with her teeth. The mother-woman wiped and wiped the little living-thing until it became clean, and then wrapped it in a piece of fabric woven of soft fibers.

Uraúka rested all that day, until the next day dawned. Then she went out to do her normal work.

But when the father-man of the new child arrived, the women

took care of him, as was the custom. The father-man had to rest for many, many days. Lying on his hanging hammock, he let the women tend to him and do his work. Very light food was prepared for the father-man; no fish or strong-roots were allowed. Tumayana came every day to bring a drink made of *Kaxiwera* and *Nauekiezi* to clean the stomach of the father-man. (*Kaxiwera* was a small-long red fruit which burned the tongue and the inside of the mouth.) The father-man had to rest for a long time from the labor of producing a new life. Uraúka did her ordinary work with the little ball of flesh hanging on her breasts, suckling.

And the days passed.

It was Uraúka's mother-woman who saw first that the little boy had nothing in his eyes. They were empty.

The father-man continued swinging at rest in his hanging hammock.

The mother-woman showed the little boy's empty-eyes to Uraúka without saying anything. She did not need to. Uraúka knew. Uraúka knew what she had to do.

When the afternoon fell gently and the shadows moved things, separating them from their dark bodies, Uraúka left the village quietly, holding her tiny burden tightly against her breast. The young woman went to the water-that-runs, which sings a burbling song in the midst of the plants. Uraúka sat with her baby boy on the edge of the water-that-runs, and rocked the little ball of flesh in her arms, and rocked. . . . Uraúka's eyes filled with the water-that-runs-from-within, from way inside where things hurt people. The water-that-runs-from-within wet Uraúka's face and ran down, down. . . .

Then, when Uraúka saw that the piece-of-humanity was sleeping deeply, she immersed the tiny being in the water-that-runs-from-outside, and held him there until the little bubbles that came up stopped rising.

Then the young woman took the limp, purple little-burden from the water, and with a groan deep from within her breast she carried the bundle-of-flesh to a place below a beautiful flowering plant. She dug with a stick, made a deep hole, planted the seed-of-man inside it, and covered it with dirt.

Uraúka, who was looking at things from within her enchantment, returned to the village with a still face and eyes which were shining from the water-that-runs-from-within, from way inside where things hurt people.

The next day Uraúka returned to her work. The young woman kneaded a dough of yellow flour, and into the dough dripped milk which was very, very white.

A sticky redness, which smelled sweet and attracted the wild beasts of the forest, streamed from smashed and strewn bodies in the middle of the green-plants. The beasts arrived, at first distrustful, and then with uninhibited gluttony and no more fear. They tore at the bodies and dragged away pieces, cleaning the bones. In a short time nothing would remain to tell the story of the terrified women whom the fear-that-drives had carried into the forest.

But the smooth-men had made a mistake, a great and terrible mistake. In their haste to go away with the women who survived, they had not looked carefully enough at the bodies they had left strewn on the ground in the forest.

One woman named Dioraná had lost her hair and a part of the skin of her head, but she lived. Terror of the wild animals of the forest, and the incredible fear-that-drives which seems to guard the exit from life and the entrance to death, made Dioraná run. She ran blind with terror and shock, and without knowing the path, but always, always kept running.

The men of the shell-mound went into the forest with their spears, searching, searching. The first day they had no luck. Lighting a fire of dry branches to keep away the wild animals, they slept at the edge of some water, waiting for the day to lighten.

When the light came, the men continued into the forest, searching for traces and footsteps, anything to indicate the path followed by the straw-men.

They searched and searched, and finally found. They found a terrified woman who dragged herself along exhausted, almost without energy: Dioraná. And Dioraná spoke. She told how the spirit-men had taken off their straw bodies and their faces of painted wood, and had turned into dark-smooth-men just like the dark-smooth-men who wore beautifully colored feathers and traded things with the village on the beach.

The shell-mound men knew then that Aramoke and his group had drawn the men away from the village on purpose, to steal the women. They knew, too, that those were the unknown strange-men who had crept around the shell-mound and taken away Ima and Malaí. They understood everything.

Karincai heard Dioraná, Tagima heard Dioraná, Kotia—Kotiatí each heard Dioraná.

The men turned their steps back to the village on the beach. On the path they met the others who had returned from the angry-waters in the trunks-that-float, and had also come to search for the women.

Then Ua heard Dioraná, and Kaúma, the chief fisherman, also heard Dioraná.

Now everybody knew.

In the village, the Great Council met on the shell-mound to resolve the greatest problem of all the great problems which men had encountered.

Dioraná told the men that all the women had fled, and that the straw—feather-men had hit and hit them until almost all of them were dead. A few had survived, and had been taken away.

Kotia spoke: "We don't know where the living-women are, but we do know an important thing: We know that the straw-men are the feather-men.

"But Aramoke, the chief with the colorful feathers, who comes to trade things without carrying weapons of attack, does not know what the shell-mound men know!" spoke Kotia.

"Thus we only need to wait until Aramoke and his group return, as they always return, to trade."

Karincai spoke: "Aramoke will never return!"

Kotiatí spoke: "The feather-men do not know that the straw-men are no longer straw-men. They will return."

Ua spoke: "Aaargh!" and gestured with his enormous hands, making the noise of crushed bones. Ua was furious!

Kotia spoke: "Malaí is alive, Ima is alive. Almost all the other women are dead. The smooth-men took a few women, and will want more. Now all the men of the village know. But Aramoke does not know! Aramoke will return."

The Great Council decided that when the weaponless feather-men came, the shell-mound men would seize Aramoke and trade the smooth-chief for the living-women.

When the Great Council ended, the men knew that there would be a fight. But first they had to find the women, and they had to be clever, just as Aramoke had been clever. Aramoke had fooled the shell-mound men. The shell-mound men had to fool Aramoke. Once they had discovered the living-women, they had to crush the colorful-men who carried no weapons. Now those men were no longer trustworthy. Until the shell-mound men did away with the smooth-men, there would be no security.

Ua spoke: "The many men decorated with colored feathers have no courage! The decorated-men go around without weapons of attack, and hide themselves in bodies-of-straw to steal women. The feather-men are weak!"

Karincai spoke: "The feather-men kill only women. They do not fight with men. They rob women stealthily. They have no courage!"

When the Great Council ended, the beach-men were sure they were stronger and braver. They thought of Aramoke's bird-men as plumed-beasts, decorated and without claws.

Aramoke was very angry with Makuré, Ikanoa, and the others who had lost the women. Aramoke's good idea would no longer work. The men of the shell-mound would not leave their women alone in the village anymore. Now there would have to be a fight. If the men had done a good job, if they had been more careful, it would not have been necessary to fight. Aramoke's village could not lose people. The lineage of smooth-men, strong in battle, had much courage and had already defeated many other tribes. But the dark-men were also clever. Aramoke said that men always ought to learn from the wild animals of the forest. Wild animals were only courageous after they were clever.

Before Aramoke's time, the forest-village had had many great dead warriors. Now the smooth-chief said: "Better great living warriors!"

It was Paleko who said, "The idea is not lost. The feather-men are still friends of the men of the beach. It will again be time to take beautifully colored feathers and stones to the great-sand, and to trade."

Paleko explained. Aramoke and his group were friends. The shell-mound men trusted Aramoke. They were no longer afraid of the beautiful decorations. When they put down their spears to gather together the stones and feathers, the smooth-men could attack and kill them all. Then they could invade the village.

* * *

The great-sand had such open clarity that it seemed to suck up the whole day in its tiny-grains. It even seemed that the eye-of-fire was a big open egg which had dug a hole in the sky up above. It was the yolk, and it had broken below and spread out in the great-sand, which was the white-light part of the egg.

The eyes of Aramoke and his decorated-men became dark from so much light when they stepped onto the light-sand. They took some time opening-closing their eyes until they became used to the brilliance of the great-sand.

The feather-men walked a short distance to the place where they were accustomed to wait until they were seen by the shell-mound men. The smooth-men carried their festive sharpened-rods hidden in tubes on their backs, and the curved-rods in their hands.

Catumai–Dao-dao, the little boys, were on the edge of the forest near the village. They climbed tall-plants to gather fruit. Catumai climbed high-high, tore off fruit, and threw it down from above *(plop!)*. Dao-dao gathered it together.

Catumai threw it *(plop, plop!)*, and Dao-dao collected it.

It was Catumai who saw them from above.

He saw Aramoke and his feathered-men, slid down the trunk all at once *(zip!)*, and, with Dao-dao behind him, ran to warn everyone.

Catumai–Dao-dao talked and made gestures, warning, warning.

Karincai took up his spear, Ua took up his spear, and Tagima and Kaúma and Kotia–Kotiatí and everyone-everyone took up their spears.

The women went into the huts, and some men stayed on guard, attentive.

Others went to meet Aramoke, with feigned-faces, which were really not their own, on top of their real faces. The men feigned opened-faces on top, but had terrible closed-faces below their feigned-faces.

When they came close to Aramoke and his group, they saw that the plumed and colorful festive-beasts did not have weapons, only tufts of feathers on their backs and big rods without points, tied with cord, in their hands.

Kotia greeted Chief Aramoke with his feigned-face. Aramoke opened his arms and bared his wide chest. The face below Kotia's feigned-face ground its teeth.

Aramoke ordered his men to put down in the sand a net full of beautiful stones which let off flashes of brilliance and seemed to have small eyes-of-fire inside them.

Aramoke's men waited for the shell-mound men to put down their weapons to examine the pretty stones. But they did not do it. Ua, Karincai, and Tagima came closer to Aramoke and made a circle around the smooth-chief.

The feather-men who were farther away still waited.

The men-of-the-beach took some steps forward with their spears and separated the plumed-chief from his group.

The feather-men were confused. Why did the hairy-men not look at the beautiful, brilliant stones which emitted flashes of eyes-of-fire?

Kotia spoke to Aramoke: "The shell-mound men want their women, all the living-women! Let the other men go get them. Aramoke stay. Living-women, living-Aramoke. No women, dead-Aramoke!"

The feather-men woke up from their shock and came forward, taking their weapons from within their tubes. But the sharpened-rods of the feather-men had to pass between the curved-rods and the cords, and the shell-mound men did not give them time. They advanced with their spears and attacked the feather-men.

Aramoke wanted to flee, and run. Ua, the great hunter, lifted his spear and threw it hard against the smooth chest which Aramoke bared as great-chief. The strength of Ua's arm made the spear enter Aramoke's chest firmly, tearing the soft-shiny skin which was painted with black lines. Red lines began to run, painting the shiny chest of Chief Aramoke.

The smooth-man then swayed on his legs. Aramoke's eyes began to imagine shadows in place of things. The great light of the eye-of-fire exploded in many points of all the colors together. It was like the arch of *Koadzi* after the water falls from the sky! Then the colors were gradually extinguished, and Aramoke was sinking into himself, sinking. . . .

Ua looked at Aramoke, whose legs had crumpled beneath him. Aramoke never knew who had thrown that sharpened-thing, which cut through the air and came flying alone to thrust itself into his chest.

The feather-men who did not fall beneath the spears had already had time to lift up their weapons and shoot sharpened-rods. Karincai looked at those incredible things with fascination.

The decorations of colored feathers suddenly had sharpened-points, and the rods without points bent in a curve when the men stretched the cords. Suddenly the feather-men had weapons pointed at the men-of-the-beach. But they were very far away! Weapons could not reach the men of the village. Not even the powerful arm of Ua had enough strength to kill from such a great distance!

Karincai blinked his eyes without believing what he was seeing. The feather-men let the cords go and the pointed-rods with feathers went off flying *(zzz)* through the air, like birds without wings, birds flying with only beak and tail. One suddenly entered Ua's body. Ua fell down doubled over!

Karincai ran; terrified, he ran. What he saw could not be true; it was something outside of things!

Tagima ran along with Karincai. He was also full of terror. But a bird-without-wings came flying and reached Tagima in the back. Karincai saw the terror stopped forever in Tagima's open eyes before he fell with his face dug into the sand, with only a cluster of colorful feathers stuck in his back like a strange and crazy ornament!

The birds-without-wings, just beak and tail, passed *(zzzz)* by Karincai's sides. It seemed that they directed themselves, these decorated-weapons of men without weapons!

Karincai kept running.

Finally the tall-plants arrived; it had seemed that they would never arrive. Crouching behind clumps of green-forest, Karincai saw from afar the white-brilliance of the great-sand full of fallen bodies.

The feather-men who survived did not come after him. They were busy picking up Aramoke's body and carrying it away.

Karincai gulped air forcefully. The agitated bird beat on the inner wall of Karincai's chest, trying to push its way out. The young man had his mouth open, and it seemed that the bird in his chest was going to rise up and flee through his mouth.

Of the men who had gone down to the beach to meet Aramoke, only Kotiatí had also escaped the horrible decorated-weapon-that-flies, which the feather-men had hidden in their clothing. Karincai thought it was good that another man was still alive. When they arrived at the village, Kotiatí told him that he had seen what Karincai had seen, or what they believed they had seen.

Did they believe it?

Karincai still did not believe what his eyes had seen. It was not the truth; it was a thing outside of things!

Karincai and Kotiatí returned, white with shock, to the village of the shell-mound.

Chapter 11

*Of how the feather-men lament and bury their dead. The
thing which is outside the order of things. Penacuai and
the lessons of the great-chief. The last journey to the village on the beach. The mark and the law of strong warriors. Colorful feathers of* Iwáulu *on the white-sand. The
feather-men and their place in the History of Man. Once
upon a time, the brave men of the shell-mounds . . .*

The shouts and cries had the same tone all through the village
of the smooth-men. The people shouted loudly, and their cries
sounded like the shrieks of a band of wild animals in the forest.
Malaí closed her ears with her hands so she would not hear the
lamentations of the men and women of the tribe. The death of
Chief Aramoke and of the other men had led to great activity in
the village, which a short time earlier had slept in the still, warm
quiet.

The men had come (it seemed) from some fight. Some were
carried, wounded or dead. Tumayana came to tend to the
wounded men. Malaí sat watching, huddled up in a corner, with
her hands on her ears. The young woman did not like the sound of

114

the constant shrieking or the repeated shouts with which the people of the village lamented their dead.

The wounded-men were stretched out on a mat woven of branches and suspended on posts pounded into the ground. They lay like this high in the air, with their wounds turned toward the bottom. Tumayana ordered dry wood to be gathered together beneath the mat of men up above, and a fire lit.

Malaí became very upset; were they cooking the men as they had the big game? Malaí looked, shocked, at those people who did things differently from Malaí's people. The young woman ran to ask Paleko, "Why are they cooking the wounded-men?"

Paleko laughed. Stupid Malaí really did not know anything! "Tumayana, the great-magician-who-cures, heats the men's wounds with the hot air of the fire to dry them. Then the evil-spirit which makes the flesh rotten can go away, and the *Iwáulu* will stop running."

Malaí, with her ears covered, looked at the men-game, whose wounds were being broiled, while Tumayana watched over them.

After a short time, men came to take the others from up on the mat and to carry them into Tumayana's hut. The magician-who-cures then spread a paste made of herbs onto the wounds of the warrior-men so they would soon be well. Tumayana said that the women should only serve them soft puddings until they were entirely healed.

The shouts and cries continued, and the men and women took off all their ornaments. They all tied just one strip around each head, and one around the belly of some of the women, to indicate that they were sad.

As soon as the end of the day arrived, the men prepared Aramoke for the Great Journey of the Spirits. The smooth-men spread shiny oil from the bark of a tree (they called it *Domalé*) over the body of the dead-chief.

Malaí wondered: "How do they do it if they don't have shells? Won't Aramoke's spirit go to the same place as the spirits of the men of the shell-mound village?"

Paleko said no. The Companion-Spirit of the smooth-men is a large feathered-beast which flies. Aramoke would be dressed in feathers for the Great Journey. They spread *Domalé* over the smooth-chief's entire body to glue on the feathers of the beast-that-flies.

Aramoke looked like an enormous white bird, with his whole

body covered with little white feathers. Malaí thought he looked pretty, the first time she had thought that about a smooth-man. He was no longer smooth, but feathered, and he had his arms open like wings. A big feather-beak was fastened on his painted-face.

The women around him let out great sighs, which grew when the men of the village rolled up the white-bird in a woven mat and tied it to an enormous pole.

Malaí was almost sad, but she was more curious. The different ways the dark-men had for doing things always made the young woman curious. Thus she had looked with her eyes at absolutely everything in the village, smelled with her nose all the smells, and let her tongue try all the tastes, curiously. Thus she had curiously passed her hand over Paleko's body, feeling in her hand his smooth-smooth body without any hair.

Ima was not curious. That was why Ima did not discover different things. She stayed glued in a corner without paying attention to anything. Kurixi (now Ima's master) had become angry. Kurixi did not like a gentle woman. That was why he poked Ima with a stick, just as he incited a wild animal of the forest, so Ima would become angry and advance at him the way Kurixi liked. The smooth-man carried the kicking woman to his hammock, and his tongue hung out in satisfaction. The wild-woman also provided Kurixi with sharpened-rods, nets, and pots, when she was lent to men who had no women. Kurixi was very clever when he settled accounts, and he was becoming the owner of many things.

The curious Malaí saw groups of men carry the package of Aramoke's mat outside the village. She knew that the burial place for the feather-men was way up above on the edge of the water-that-runs. They had to carry the man-mat on a long journey on a trunk-that-floats. The men left with the bodies of Aramoke and the other dead before *Pituna* came.

Karincai and Kotiatí arrived in the shell-mound village with their faces white with shock, and were soon surrounded by men and women. The two men spoke. The only two living-men told the tale, with the boys Catumai–Dao-dao jumping around them, men shaking their heads, women rolling their eyes, some young women hugging their children to their breasts, some younger men listening quietly. Everybody heard everything, and then they asked questions. Everybody asked questions at the same time. They wanted to know about the beast-that-flies-that-kills, the strange bird with only a beak and a tail, but no wings, which the feather-men took off their backs and set free with cords, and which came alone, flying on its own account to kill for the smooth-men. They shook their heads at such a thing, which they had never heard spoken of!

"But if this is true, if the feather-men have weapons which kill by themselves, how can the people of the shell-mound conquer the strange-men, if they cannot get close?"

Karincai spoke of Ua, of Tagima, of Kotia, and of all the others who had remained far off on the sand. The men had to go get them.

But now the men had a kind of fear which they had never felt before, a terror much greater than their fear of the evil-spirits which they had learned how to satisfy. It was a terror greater than their fear of a pack of all the wild animals which they had ever faced, even the great wild-fish of the angry-waters which had eaten Manaú's leg. This terror which the men felt now was the horror of a thing which was outside the order of things.

Kaúma and the other men went with this great fear to get the bodies of the dead-men. With their eyes searching to all sides, watching, they quickly buried Ua and his poor companions on the new shell-mound. They returned to the village all together, like a pack of astonished beasts, watching, watching, with eyes spread out to all sides.

The smooth-men ascended the water-that-runs carrying Aramoke's body rolled in a mat. They pushed back the waters with pieces of wood, pushing the hollow-trunks up and up.

They spent the whole time of *Pituna* traveling. When the eye-of-fire looked down and saw itself looking up from the eye-of-water, the men arrived in the place where they buried their dead.

On the edge of the water-that-runs, at a point where the full-water never reached, they dug a deep hole in which they put Aramoke's body, standing up and supported by a pole. Then they closed the hole with branches and big leaves from the tall-plants, and covered everything with earth. The men were sad, for Chief Aramoke had been a great, good, brave man. Ikanoa put on top of the new-earth of Aramoke's last dwelling a container full of fruits and cakes made of meal, which they had brought with them. Aramoke would still need food for a few days, until his spirit went away on the Great Journey.

Makuré ground his top and bottom teeth together and said to Aramoke, as though he were still listening, "The hairy-men will pay! Aramoke's men will now put an end to the people of the shell-mound, even without Aramoke."

The men all together said yes with one voice to the words of Makuré.

Kurixi said, "The men will acquire women, so Aramoke's village can grow strong and be full of new great-warriors!"

The men all together said yes to Kurixi's words.

Then they got into the trunks-that-float and began the journey back on the water-that-runs, for another long stretch of time. To return they did not even have to push the water with the pieces of wood. The trunks slipped along easily, following the same path as the long-sweet-water.

Makuré thought about the big strong body of Aramoke and the painted wide chest which he bared (he was a great-chief). Now, he thought, it would become just bones! Aramoke's spirit, it was true, would go to the good place where the great-warriors stay forever at the end of their battles. Makuré thought that when the time came for them to return to dig up Aramoke's body and clean the rest of his flesh from his bones with the point of a bone heated in the fire, they ought to bring to Aramoke news of the end of the shell-mound people. Only then, thought Makuré, would Aramoke's spirit be satisfied. His bones would be put into a big pot, together with his weapons as chief-warrior, and everything would be buried together forever under a beautiful tall-plant.

Pituna had already taken over the whole village in the forest when the smooth-men pulled the hollow-trunks up to the edge of the water and jumped out to the ground.

Aramoke's hut was empty. The great-chief's women and daughters had cut their hair to show that they were sad. They had gone to another hut, that of Aramoke's first-son, who was now great-chief.

Paleko and Kurixi gathered together everything that remained of the dead-chief, and burned it. Then they mixed what remained with dirt, and scattered it all around. Now the great-chief was a dead-warrior, and stories would be told of his bravery.

Aramoke's first-son was still just-a-boy. But the father-man had had time to teach his son the lessons of a great-chief. Penacuai had stayed for four risings of the long-water (a time during which the trees had flowered and then given fruit four times alone in his own hut. There he had learned to resolve the problems of the village and to do justice. Penacuai, just-a-boy, already had helped Aramoke to resolve questions of the tribe, and had received in payment sharpened-rods, stones, and beautiful ornaments worked of feathers.

The time for Penacuai to learn to be chief had ended with a great feast a short time before. The great feast for the chief-just-a-boy had had a great deal of dancing accompanied by the sounds of round trunks *(boom, boom)*, and of fine canes with holes in them *(tweet, tweet)*, great pieces of good-game, many, many gourds of strong drink, and the dance of the white-deer in which the men and women pretended to be game and hunters.

Penacuai's great moment had come when he fought the dance of the magic-fight. He was dressed in the leather-skin of the animal which has no legs and drags along in the dust, an animal which he himself had to have killed. Penacuai danced and defeated the beast-of-feathers, who was a great-warrior dressed up and pretending to be the Spirit-Companion of all the feather-men. Penacuai had to dominate the Spirit in order to become the great-chief after his father Aramoke. (All this was imagined-magic.) Only afterwards could Penacuai wear the clothing which indicated that he was the first-son and almost-chief.

Penacuai spent the good-days as boy-chief fishing in the long-water. He was so fast with his pointed-rods that as fast as the fish sparkled past, beneath his sight, their brilliance was stabbed, stopped forever. The good-days of boyhood were now gone for Penacuai. Now it was time to dance another kind of dance, that which calls the spirits-of-war to guarantee victory in a great fight, such as the one which the smooth-men had in front of them and which would be the end (they said) of the shell-mound men.

Tira, the young-woman–girl who was destined for Penacuai, had enormous eyes full of shock when she saw the men, including Penacuai, who had been of straw turn into majestic men-of-feathers. The boy-chief looked like a big bird with blue and red plumes. His face was covered with black lines, and he was terrible and beautiful like the all-powerful Spirit. Penacuai curved his enormous bow (the same size as he) with the grace of a bird which is going to fly, but what flew was the sharpened-rod which cut through the air as rapidly as a ray of light. The eye-of-fire high up above was frightened, and hid behind a swollen-white-sponge.

The shadows descended.

The feather-men, with plumed weapons and faces painted with black stripes, all set out on the last journey to the village on the beach.

Karincai saw what was left of the day creeping past in the sky tinged with red. He rapidly piled up oysters before the mouth-of-darkness let its throat go along the rocks to swallow the afternoon.

The mouth-of-darkness opened, letting out its breath, and sand ran over sand. While Karincai carried the shells to the village, the eye-of-fire rolled past in the sky above, and the darkness was complete.

The quiet village slept a light sleep. All around, the big green-plants were only one dark shadow. Kaúma was on guard.

Karincai stooped down next to Kaúma beside the hearth with its long-tongues which guarded the center of the village. The air smelled hot; the air smelled good. The darkness was very quiet. A beast-that-flies gave a short chirp, a wild beast of the forest gave a sharp scream. Then everything was quiet again.

Suddenly Kaúma stopped to listen, the air imprisoned in his chest so he could hear better. The noise of footsteps crackled lightly and cautiously in the forest beyond. Kaúma thought that it was the noise of a large beast.

Karincai pointed his ear to the side where the noise had come, but everything was equally black.

Suddenly Kaúma heard the noise of trodden leaves from the other side, and another chirp of a beast-that-flies, one short and one long. It was no longer a beast-that-flies.

Karincai's ear grew, spreading out to all sides. The chirps-yells now echoed from one side to the other, and the trodden ground crackled on all sides. Kaúma and Karincai could see nothing around them. The darkness mixed everything together. Karincai shouted for the men inside the huts, and they all came out.

Soon the men joined together in the middle of the village where the burning fire guarded the huts. Holding their spears, they waited, looking around.

But no one came.

The men saw nothing, but heard with their discriminating ears the footsteps on leaves all around them.

But no one appeared.

The fire burning in the middle of the village made the outline of their bodies around the men. From afar, over in the forest, they were easy marks, their arms and legs moving as dark shadows on the live background of the flames.

It was then that they came humming. Rapid. Accurate. They cut through the air with their bodies-without-wings (only beak and tail), thin as tubes, sure. They knocked over one by one the black outlines of moving legs and arms against the light background of the fire in the center of the village.

Kaúma looked all around at the men who fell down stunned without doing anything. The buzzing was coming from all sides. Their spears were useless in their hands. They fell without seeing anything, and heard only the buzzing flight. Kaúma looked around dizzily. They passed on all sides, above his head, beside his shoulders, below his legs, buzzing, above, below . . . and suddenly in front, right in front. Kaúma's knees doubled, and he fell.

The shadows were already shrinking and things were taking shape when Karincai saw the feather-men arriving from all sides.

Catumai–Dao-dao trembled; their skinny bones were shaking, and they shrank into a corner.

Penacuai, crowned with colorful feathers, entered majestically on the first strand of light which reached the village.

Plumed-men picked up the boys Catumai–Dao-dao without harming them, and carried them away. Inside the huts there remained only women wrapped up in the cocoon of their terror, and children who were little balls of fear and shock.

Karincai, the last man of the shell-mound, looked at Penacuai--just-a-boy dressed as great-chief, looked at the enormous curved-rod in the hand of the smooth-man, and threw his spear on the ground.

Penacuai understood. Karincai twisted his face at the boy-chief, indicating that the boy did not have the courage to come close to the man. From a distance Karincai would certainly die; a spear is of no use against the weapon-that-flies.

The two men stood facing one another. All of Penacuai's men stopped, immobile, just watching. Women put their heads out the doors of the hut and watched, fascinated. Penacuai advanced first. In the new light of morning, the thin chest of the boy-man suddenly grew in Karincai's eyes. Karincai also advanced, without fear and without a weapon. Penacuai looked in Karincai's eyes and saw the mark of a strong warrior. The eyes of warriors are all alike. They are known by their brilliance, and are respected according to their own laws. The smooth-chief looked in the eyes of the warrior, without fear of Karincai, and threw his curved-rod on the ground. The great bird with feathers advanced its unarmed body and fought with the last man of the shell-mound before Aramoke's spirit, just as he had fought with the Great Spirit before the whole village in the forest.

The body with hair and the body with feathers then rolled over one another along the ground of white-sand. Karincai's body was a sturdy trunk. The boy-chief was a thin rod which could pliantly double over. Karincai came hard and heavy. Penacuai slid rapidly and lightly.

In the track made by their bodies along the path feathers were dropped, and more feathers . . . a red thread ran on the white-sand.

The bodies rolled around in the fascinated eyes of the men and women.

A red-eye opened on the white-sand, a little pool. One body lay stretched out on the ground. The other got up against the light sky. The eye-of-fire appeared up above.

Penacuai, the boy-chief, could return to the village in the forest with his prisoners of war. He could return for the great final ceremony for his father-man. He would take with him peace for the spirit of Chief Aramoke, women who would continue the great, strong race of the feather-man, and children as well.

The dark-smooth-men followed their trail in the History of Man, without looking back at their steps.

In the village on the beach there was no one else to bury the bodies which had fallen beside the shell-mound. But Time slowly spread a fine layer over those people who had been alive, who had been human beings. Time covered everything. Below, even now, they are there in the middle of the shell-mounds, all of them: Tagima, Kaúma, Karincai, Ua, Kotia–Kotiatí the two equal-brothers . . . all.

The feather-men survived.

For a very long time the feather-men were the masters of the earth, until one day, from the angry-waters, came the men-of-cloth.

THE SAMBAQUI CULTURE

Seven or eight thousand years ago the sambaquis (shell middens) which are situated today on the island of Santo Aramo were located on two different islands of what is now called the Paleo-Archipelago of Santos. Today that archipelago has been reduced to only some larger islands, such as São Vicente, Santo Amaro, and Baixado Santista (the Engá-Guassu of the Indians), next to the base of the Serra do Mar. Both the Serra do Mar and the archipelago were formed by eolic and marine sedimentation. Several islands were joined together by this same geomorphological process.

Our shell-mound people lived on Santo Amaro in two villages which are only about fourteen kilometers apart, but which were at that time separated by the sea. This story tries to re-create the daily life of these people, the way in which they lived, and their beliefs and rituals. We work from a solid research base, but with free use of resources of imagination and language, in an attempt to discover the human image of this little-known people. We seek to find again, through the literary word, the spontaneous and sensitive living beings which they certainly were.

The people who inhabited the sambaquis in the area of Santos, Iguape, and Cananéia lived in these places between three thousand and ten thousand years ago. They were dark brown with a yellowish cast, and did not have Mongoloid traits. They were of a more North Asian type, perhaps Siberian. They were ignorant of pottery, systematic agriculture, or the domestication of any species of animal, even the dog which the Indians of that time knew. They lived principally by gathering and fishing, with very little hunting. They did not have powerful flinging tools such as the

bow or the sling; consequently, hunting of land animals was sec-
ondary, and perhaps done only with traps.

They knew thread, however, and if they did not yet weave,
they did spin fibers of embira, pita or agave, tucum, and other
fibrous plants which are fairly abundant on the shore, making a
thick thread with which they sewed skins or trunk bark, or fastened on rough buttons of bone or wood. They perhaps made
fishing nets, which Hans Staden, Lery, and others observed from
the earliest days of colonization. Spindles and bone needles used
by the shell-midden people have been found at Mar Casado and
Maratuá, proving that they knew how to spin.

They worked very well in stone, which they polished. Their
tools were limited to various sizes of bifacial or unifacial hand
axes of granite, diabase, basalt, or gneiss. Some of the hand axes
which have been found are whole, and carefully polished. Several
of the smaller ones have holes, suggesting that they were insigina
or armaments.

They knew how to capture big animals such as the capybara
and jaguar, certainly by means of traps. The presence of whales in
the sambaquis is explained by the frequency with which this ceta-
cean is grounded on beaches (an occurrence noted from the six-
teenth century to the present). Large fish, including several
species of shark, frequented the shallow waters, and were certainly wounded with long sharpened spears of bamboo or wood.
Other fish were hunted with smaller spears, possibly of bamboo,
on whose ends teeth were fastened like fishhooks. Spears similar
to those are still used today by the natives on the coast of Vene-
zuela and on Florida Island in the Pacific.

They may already have been sedentary or semisedentary.

The people of the sambaquis probably imported or went else-
where to find the basalt and diabase for their stone axes, because
only a very small quantity of basalt was found in situ on the island
of Santo Amaro. It is also possible that they traded for it with
other tribes.

Polishing was done with sand and water, by scraping with a
piece of wood for a long period of time in a monotonous and
unhurried manner: "soft sand and water on hard stone . . ." They
made holes in animal teeth in this way. This technique has been
observed in studies of comparative ethnology and has been demonstrated in re-creations.

Objects made of teeth, horn, and bones of fish, birds, and

mammals (especially small ones) and of whales and river dolphins are abundant in the shell middens.

An upside-down whale carcass is found at the base of many shell middens, leading us to conclude that the enormous amount of food supplied by a beached whale was considered to be a gift from the spirits, and attributed to the magic which rules primitive peoples, including the shell-mound people. Thus, such an event would lead to the building of a new shell mound.

What are the sambaqui? (Sambaqui is a name which according to anthropologists has various explanations. Its etymology is most likely that suggested by Teodoro Sampáio: *Tamba + Qui* = "Pile of Shells.")

The sambaqui are formations of marine shells, generally located along the seashore. But there are also shell middens in the interior, along the edges of great and small rivers. The shells for these middens come from river mollusks, and even terrestrial ones (like the snail). The stratification of the sambaquis is well defined; it consists of irregular layers of oysters, mussels (anomalocardia brasiliana), or other mollusks such as Madiolus and Phacaides. Burials are found between these layers of shells. Some are well characterized, with human bones and remains, the remains and fragments of mammals, reptiles, and birds, and stone tools.

Because these burial places were not dug in natural earth, the stratigraphy of the shell midden is determined by layers of carbon and ashes (showing the existence of primitive funeral rites), enormous stone hearths, burned bones and stones, and other details.

There are layers of empty oyster shells, which indicates that their contents were used beforehand. We know that these mollusks, along with fish, formed the basis of alimentation for the sambaqui people. But layers of mussels were frequently deposited whole, without the food having been consumed.

Why did they work to collect the food, and then abandon it intact?

Most of the human bones are found in this layer, some in formal burials. Tools and animal remains, as well as traces of hearths, are also found here.

Rigorous investigations carried out by the São Paulo Institute of Prehistory, on the island of Santo Amaro, Canal de Bertioga, Piaçaguera and Cananéia, clarify this point for us.

The shell midden was not a necropolis, but a resting place for significant individuals (chiefs, perhaps) and their families. It is possible that prisoners were sacrificed to be buried with those individuals, since the bones demonstrate visible anthropomorphic differences. Brachicephalous skulls, without the rest of their skeletons, were found at Maratuá next to the whole skeletons of the dolicocephalous types buried there. In Mar Casado the skeletons are accompanied by very fragmented pieces of human bones, in a clear enough vestige of anthropophagia (or cannibalism). Anthropophagia is a magic ritual consisting of the ingestion of the power, the courage, the goodness, and all the qualities of the dead, or part of them, in a form of "communicating the victim." This was perhaps a primitive rite later smoothed over by the Catholic religion, but keeping the same intensity. We know, through studies of the origin of religions and of primitive people, that rituals are never invented, but are inherited or substituted, and have evolved in an uninterrupted sequence from the earliest times of humanity.

Verifying this thesis, we remember that a short time ago Indians in the north of Brazil devoured, soon after his death, a priest who had been everything to them for dozens of years. The priest had been their spiritual father, their protector, and the provider of food and medicine. They felt unprotected and abandoned following his death. The explanation they gave to the civilized white man at the inquest which followed was that it was only by devouring the priest in this way that they could keep him eternally with them. And in a form of defense they said that the priest also swallowed his "Father" every morning. The sentiment which moved them was the same, as was the respect.

The utensils and belongings next to the skeletons on Maratuá tell us that these people were buried with everything they possessed. The presence of red ocher on the bones shows us traces of theur beliefs. (Even today in Brazil, Indians like the Kraós paint dead bodies with a red dye plant, arnolto. Similar use of red ocher has been observed all over the world since the Paleolithic era.) These rituals can be interpreted today, almost without margin of error, by the comparative anthropologist, for there are still primitives living in the same magic-ritual stage in which the shell-midden people lived then. This re-creation shows us a very interesting world, rich in imagination and originality. Often, as well, it gives us an explanation of civilized customs whose origins we never even suspected!

There are no traces of habitations in the shell middens. There could not have been dwellings on them. The village would be to the side. Traces of sedentary life should be sought in neighboring areas a short distance away. The Sambaqui must have lived in shacks or huts which were very crude, but which protected them from dampness and mosquitoes.

Primitive men, possessing only inferior Neolithic tools, faced a painful and difficult life on a wild coast in the midst of bogs and mosquitoes. They had to kill wild beasts from up close, because they lacked propelled tools; they were tortured by spiders, snakes, ants, mosquitoes, gnats, ticks, and wasps, which perhaps bothered them more than the wild animals; they had to confront various poisonous snakes and spiders; and they breathed the methane from the bogs and the organic decomposition of the shell middens themselves, which were permeable. These were the surroundings in which the Sambaqui existed. Today not even the roughest peoples would stand for it.

The shell midden was a multiple social center, the place for group meetings, a great kitchen and living room for the clan, the totemic monument of Paleo-American man. Its location did not occur by chance, but according to certain conditions imposed, at least principally, by magic factors. It was a funeral monument, but not a necropolis. It was the resting place for prominent individuals, a few or many chiefs and leaders of the clan, possibly even of tribes from which our Indians could have originated. Collective joys and sorrows were commemorated there. The magic rites were carried out there as in the European Magdalene caverns or later in the immense temples and vast tombs of Egypt and Mesopotamia.

Each layer of the shell midden corresponds to a determined group or a determined generation, or possibly to a dynasty, if such terms can be used in reference to primitive groups. Once a prominent person or persons died, the body would be deposited on a layer of mollusk shells and covered with another layer, this time of another mollusk, which would be the totem of the group. This totem would be naturally chosen by its alimentary function, demonstrated by the quantity of existing mollusks which would be placed there intact or in part. These mollusk-totems would completely cover the mortal remains of the person, to protect him, to guard the dead, to make the burial inviolate, and even to assure food for the Great Journey.

These rituals were proved, by chance, by Paul Rivet in Chile, when he was invited by natives to a banquet on the high base of a sambaqui, where a primitive group cooked oysters on a great fire lit in that place. Each one of the feasters took a shell, ate its contents, and threw the shell behind him, without looking. They told him that they also buried their dead there.

The presence of mollusks as funeral ornaments is not rare among primitives. In various parts of the world, skulls surrounded by actual headdresses of these little animals have been found. In Brazil the skull from Maratuá, nicknamed "Miss Sambaqui," was riddled with dozens of tiny shells stuck and fossilized on the bones of the skull. It can be seen in the São Paulo Institute of Prehistory.

One can believe that the shell-midden people were totemic. Totemism precedes religion. The totem is not a god, but a guide, a well-doer, a protecting companion. Most totems are revered in magic ceremonies, so that the tribe will be provided with food and necessary things. Each tribe tries to multiply its totem, for the well-being of the community. Frequently the rites consist of imitation of the desired effects. This is what is called homeopathic or imitative magic. The shell-midden people carried out ceremonies accumulating oysters so there would be an abundance of food.

The sociological glue of totemism was magic. It was the remedy against fears, a means of preserving life, principally against unknown powers which are manifested by phenomena inexplicable to primitives: thunder, rain, wind, and so forth. All the activities of primitive people are tied to magic rituals. Magic tells them not only what they ought to do, but what they ought not to do: positive precepts are enchantments, negative ones are taboos. Positive magic is also known as witchcraft.

All the rites described in this book pertain to these categories of magic and totemism. They were, or are in some form, practiced by primitives who have a cultural identity with the Sambaqui. This working hypothesis is accepted as valid in the field of comparative anthropology.

Due to studies in comparative ethnology we know the totemic rites of various tribes of North America, Australia, and Oceania, principally those of passage, adolescence, and other social-magic rites.

The Sambaqui, who did not know the bow or pottery, would have been crushed by a group with a superior culture which arrived thousands of years later, better armed and more evolved.

Such a group (or groups) were the antecedents of our Indians, or
some of them, coming by way of the North or Central Pacific or
Asiatic, Siberian, or Polynesian migrations.

How can this hypothesis be proven?

The Botocudos were the only primitive group treated in a hos-
tile way by the other groups found by the Portuguese. They were
called *Tapuias,* which means "the enemy." The skulls of the Botocudos have characteristics in common with those of Lagoa
Santo and those found in the shell middens. There is a hypothesis
that these were the last direct descendants of shell-midden people.
They were destroyed by more avanced and better-armed Indians
who arrived later. The Botocudos had bows and arrows and baked
clay, but these skills could have been obtained later, by accultura-
tion, just as the Indians learned, by the same process, to bury
their dead in the shell middens (which can be observed in the
upper layers).

Were the Xetás, driven back to the confines of Paraná, the last
descendants of the Botocudos, thought to be extinct?

Only the study of important prehistoric sites will one day give
us definitive answers to all these questions. Many things remain
to be discovered about the Sambaqui and their culture. The con-
frontation of this culture with that of the pre-Indian, its conqueror,
becomes very interesting. In this area we already have material
for study which is much more vast and precise, and which in-
cludes traditions and customs which remain alive in our time. All
the facts and events which make up this story were taken from
reality, from all the documentation at our reach. For example, the
final fight of this narrative actually happened between the Karajá
and Tapirapé Indians at the beginning of this century. (It was
described by the anthropologist Fritz Krause.) We know that this
type of war has been waged from time to time since prehistory.

If the "men of the shell mound" did not have precise words to
name each thing, the "feather-men" already possessed a specific
vocabulary. With it they grow before our eyes as another people,
no less beautiful and moving, alive and human.

But perhaps we do not have much time to study our "feather-
men." They too are coming to an end, persecuted by the culture
and technology of white men. However, there is a difference between reality and our fiction: There is no hope that the women
and children will be saved. The culture shock, now, is too great.

Extinction will be total.

Nheengatu Vocabulary
Included in the Text

Anikê: hen
Anikexi: hen's eggs
Bolobedo: parakeet, parrot
Cuaçu: deer
Domalé: gum resin
Iauráete: tiger (jaguar)
Iwáulu: red color
Ixiulani: bluish fruit
Kaxiwera: hot pepper
Koadzi: rainbow
Kodoni: turtle
Kodonizi: turtle eggs
Macacaitá: monkey
Maeréboe: eternal spirit
Nauekiezi: honey
Pirauaçu: whale
Pituna: night
Tabolá: wax
Tapiira: capybara
Tijuu-Holo-Larari: eclipse
Ualú: gourd rattle

Biographical Note

Stella Maria Whitaker Carr Ribeiro was born in Guanabara and now lives and works in São Paulo. Her poetry was first published in 1965 by Cassiano Ricardo, and she became well known as a member of the "1960s generation." *Sambaqui,* her first novel, was originally published in 1975.

She comes from a long line of writers and journalists. Among her ancestors was the legendary Cavaleiro Roberto Carr Ribeiro, a special magistrate for the King of Portugal during the time of Gomes Freire de Andrade and a member of the Select Academy which met in Rio de Janeiro in 1752. Her grandfather, Eduardo Carr Ribeiro, was one of the founders of the republican newspaper *O Povo,* along with Albeto Torres. Her father, whom Sergio Miliet called a minor poet even though he never published a book of poetry, was a journalist. He also wrote and translated several books on organization theory, a discipline which he helped to introduce in Brazil. She was also related to João Carr Ribeiro Pena, a São Paulo journalist who served as a London correspondent for *Folhas* and whose premature disappearance is greatly regretted.

Stella Carr Ribeiro has had some experience as a journalist for *Jornal de Letras,* for which she wrote a column in which she tried to bring together writers and literary movements from all over Brazil. From this short experiment she acquired friends from all over the country: from Amazonas, Goiás, Paraíba, from the north and south. These friendships long outlasted the short life of her column.

She was the director and vice president of the Brazilian Union of Writers and was an active participant in the cultural life of São Paulo. She worked with Editora Jose Olympio to coordinate conferences and contacts between writers and São Paulo students, seeking to establish dialogue between writers and young people, their potential readers.

After the death of her son, Stella Carr Ribeiro abandoned active participation in the cultural scene, but not literature. She has been writing children's books for the past few years.

Sambaqui is a novel based on one of the great passions of her life: anthropology. She became enthusiastic about the subject when she took the first course which Paulo Duarte, recently arrived from the Museum of Man in Paris, gave in São Paulo. The course was given at the auditorium of *Folhas,* which in the early 1960s sponsored a variety of cultural programs. She followed Duarte to the Municipal Library where she took classes in anthropology and prehistory. Finally, when the Institute of Prehistory was established at the University of São Paulo, she spent time there gathering material for this book.